STILL IN LOVE

DELANEY DIAMOND

GARDEN AVENUE PRESS

Still in Love by Delaney Diamond

Copyright © 2015, Delaney Diamond

Garden Avenue Press

Atlanta, Georgia

ISBN: 978-1-940636-22-1 (Paperback edition)

ISBN: 978-1-940636-33-7 (Ebook edition)

To all of you wonderful readers who followed this story every Friday as each episode was revealed, chatted with me on the blog, shared your comments on Facebook and Twitter, or sent an email letting me know your thoughts.
I enjoyed each and every conversation and appreciated your feedback. I miss our Fridays together. We'll have to do it again real soon.

CHAPTER 1

*C*oming back to Argentina had not been anywhere near on Nadine Alesini's list of things to do, but when her former sister-in-law followed up a wedding invitation with a personal plea, she hadn't been able to say no. Now, at least for the moment, she was glad she hadn't.

She'd missed Buenos Aires.

The "Paris of South America" had been her home for twelve years, eleven of those while married. Her marriage had ended, but the product of their union sat close to her side outside the Ezeiza International Airport terminal. Antonella, her twelve-year-old daughter, whose voluminous black curls were piled on top of her head in a high ponytail, sat with feet swinging as her eyes searched the cars pulling up to the curb.

The eleven-hour flight hadn't diminished her daughter's excitement one iota. The annual flights south were not enough for Antonella, and this bonus trip for the wedding had made her ecstatic; she'd get to see her father and the rest of her family twice in one year.

Nadine tucked her chin-length hair behind an ear, and —like her daughter—searched the cars for her ex-husband. Where her daughter practically bounced with excited energy, a knot of anxiety lay heavy in her stomach.

"What time is it?" Antonella asked.

Nadine checked the face of her phone. "A few minutes after six. He's not that late."

Antonella sighed. "He's usually on time."

Behind a red sports car, a black limo approached, and Nadine knew it was Cortez even before the door opened. Not only because it was a limo, but because her skin prickled, as if someone had dusted wool fabric along her arms and created static electricity, and the hairs stood on end, a clear indication of his presence.

The car cruised to a stop, and the back door opened before the driver could come around to it. Cortez Alesini emerged, looking quite relaxed in a pair of dark shades. He was dressed casually in black slacks and a plain white shirt, which looked anything but plain the way it lay against his tanned skin and hugged his muscular chest and arms.

"Papá!"

Antonella raced forward and jumped into his outstretched arms.

Nadine stood, gaze pinned on Cortez's bent head as he lifted their daughter from the ground and crushed her to him. Their close, affectionate embrace created a tightness of guilt in her chest, and she looked away, reaching for the luggage. Before she could even touch her suitcase, the driver, Joachim, grabbed the handle.

"I have it, *señora*." Joachim was in his early fifties but

appeared fifteen years younger. Along with his uniform of a tan shirt and dark trousers, he wore an ever-present smile and had a self-effacing manner, often bowing his head to demonstrate his respect.

He took off with the bags, leaving Nadine to stand awkwardly, waiting, as Cortez and Antonella finished their greeting. When he finally released her, Antonella held onto his hand, behaving more like a two-year-old than a twelve-year-old. The way she clung to her father once again created a pain in Nadine's chest, reminding her that she was the reason they had to live apart.

Cortez removed his sunglasses, almost as if in slow motion, and Nadine felt the full strength of his gaze, like a blow to her chest. Her breath held for a beat, rendering her motionless, tightening every muscle in her body. In that moment, she was very much like one of his millions of adoring fans. Transfixed. Thrilled, that of all the people hurrying by, he'd chosen to lavish her with his attention.

Finally she found her voice. "Hello, Cortez. It's been a long time."

Three years, in fact, since they'd last seen each other in person. Their split had been less than amicable, and in all that time she'd only seen the odd photo of him online, but mostly the photos she did see were pictures Antonella shared after each trip. By silent, mutual agreement, their only contact was by phone or email. Elsa, her former sister-in-law, had been the one to escort Antonella south every year on a chartered flight.

"Nadine." *Nah-deen.* He and his entire family said her name the same way, using a lyrical, almost poetic pronunciation. But his voice…God, his voice was like the gentle strum of a guitar—deep and enticing, and made her want to lean into the sound.

His eyes roamed over her, gaze lingering on her breasts and skimming her hips, before dropping lower to her denim-clad thighs. The thorough examination left her tingling all over.

"You have not changed much," he murmured, almost to himself.

The warm-sounding compliment made her heart ache. This was what she'd been dreading ever since her decision to come—the face-to-face with Cortez and having to endure the emotions he'd evoke.

"Neither have you, so we're even."

He'd been a gorgeous young man, in every sense of the word, and as an older, mature-looking man, he could clearly still turn heads. His eyes, gray with hints of blue, showed signs of wrinkles at the corners, but age had simply ripened his looks, giving him a more distinguished appearance.

Tall and very broad, Cortez was half-Italian and half-Argentine, and exemplified what could happen when two equally attractive people fell in love and procreated. His father had come to the country as part of a wave of Italian and Spanish immigrants from Europe and fallen in love with Cortez's mother. They married and proceeded to have a large family of three boys and three girls.

"I think you must be blind." A sexy smile lifted one side of his mouth. During the height of his popularity as a recording artist, that same expression had been duplicated on posters and advertisements around the continent, plastered on the walls of teenaged girls, and made the hearts of women of every ethnicity go pitter-patter. "I

have many more gray hairs since the last time I saw you."
He touched a hand to his silky hair.

Now that he was no longer in the public eye and
hounded by adoring fans, he'd allowed his hair to grow a
little longer, the curling mass dusting his collar and ears.
Silver around the temples indicated middle age had
caught up with him, but by his fit body and trim waist, he
might have been caught, but not yet conquered.

"I wouldn't worry too much about it," Nadine said.
"You look fine."

They stared at each other, the moment a little
awkward, and the air becoming thick and soupy with the
burden of unspoken thoughts. Right as Cortez opened his
mouth to talk, Antonella tugged his hand, drawing their
attention and slamming the door on whatever was tran-
spiring between them.

"Let's go, Papá. I'm ready to see everybody."

One would think Antonella hadn't been here just six
months before, but she'd lived in Argentina the first nine
years of her life, and though she'd become acclimated to
the United States very quickly, she loved her home
country and her family one hundred times more.

Cortez's face softened, filling with affection as he
looked at his daughter. "After you, *mi amor*."

Antonella hurried into the back of the vehicle, and
Cortez extended an arm toward the open door. "After
you," he said to Nadine.

"Thank you."

She slid past him and climbed into the plush interior.
She settled onto the leather seat beside Antonella, and
Cortez joined them, sitting with his back to the front.

"Are you taking me to Elsa's first?" Nadine asked, setting her purse on the seat next to her.

Her sister-in-law had offered to let Nadine stay in one of the bedrooms of her three-bedroom condo.

"Didn't she tell you?" Cortez frowned at her.

"Tell me what?"

"You're staying at the house."

Nadine's heart jolted at the news. "I—I don't understand. Elsa said I'd be staying at her place."

Cortez crossed his legs and extended a hand across the back of the leather seat. "Change of plans. Two of her close college girlfriends who originally couldn't make it were able to come and they're staying at her condo. She asked me if you could stay at the house, and I told her that was fine. That's not a problem, is it?"

"No, of course not." Unless one considered a week in the same house as her ex-husband a problem.

Nadine was very aware of Antonella's presence, and she didn't want to give the impression that they couldn't get along.

"Gustavo and his family will be coming to stay for the wedding," Cortez said, referring to his older brother, "but there's plenty of room at the house."

"I know. I used to live there." Nadine wished she could pull back the words. She'd meant to only state a fact but had sounded bitchy instead.

A muscle in his cheek twitched. "Yes, you did." The words sounded like an indictment of wrongdoing rather than a simple statement.

Abruptly, he shifted his attention to Antonella. "How was the trip, *mi amor*?"

They lapsed into Spanish to continue the conversation.

As the vehicle rolled toward the gated community where Cortez lived, impending dread rode along in Nadine's stomach. She wondered how she'd make it through the next seven days without falling apart, in a house she used to live in, with the man she used to love.

CHAPTER 2

*C*ortez slipped back on his sunglasses. While he carried on a conversation with his daughter, he kept an eye on his wife—*ex*-wife. After all this time, one would think his brain would have grown accustomed to the fact that she was no longer his spouse, but every now and again he slipped up. She had been his first wife—should have been his only wife—but anger and mutual pain had caused irreparable damage in their marriage and torn them apart.

She hardly looked her forty years, wearing a loose-fitting shirt with billowing long sleeves, a pair of jeans that molded to round hips—meant for a man's hands to hold onto—and thick thighs to lose himself between. Then there was her incredible ass, which he hadn't been able to resist ogling as she moved past him to enter the car.

His fingers folded tightly into his palm, and he resolved not to be distracted by her appearance, no matter how unbearable it was to be this close and not able to touch.

He'd almost declined his sister's request to have Nadine stay at the house, but Elsa had pleaded with him because she'd promised Nadine she wouldn't have to worry about the cost of lodging if she came for the wedding. Yet in the midst of all the preparations, she had clearly forgotten to pass on the message to Nadine about the change of plans.

The limo paused at the security gate of Nortada, located on the outskirts of Buenos Aires, and one of the first communities of its kind in Argentina. They rolled through the entrance, past the first of nine neighborhoods that occupied the affluent enclave filled mostly with upper-middle-class families, but also wealthy business-people and celebrities.

A family of ducks waddled across the street—not an unusual sight in this peaceful environment—to get to the man-made lake on the other side. The purple blooms of jacaranda trees lined the road and fought to wrestle attention from the bright yellow of the lemon trees, whose fragrance could be detected even through the car's barrier of glass and steel.

They'd chosen this place as their home because of the numerous amenities which ensured residents could have all their needs satisfied within the gates. Not only did they have their own medical center, the sports center offered rugby, soccer, American football, and tennis. A mall offered a below-ground supermarket, with clothing and small restaurants occupying the upper two floors. Then there were four private schools, one of which was the bilingual Catholic school Antonella had attended before she and her mother moved to the States. Over the years, he and his former bandmates from Los Tigres had put on shows at the performing arts center to raise funds used to preserve and maintain the community's green space.

Life at Nortada was truly utopian living, which many on the outside complained was elitist and provided an unrealistic view of the world for the children raised within its borders. But during the height of his performing career, he'd seen it as the perfect place to raise a family and the privacy and security put his mind at ease when he traveled, except now he had to endure the tranquil landscape alone. His carefully constructed paradise was nothing more than a glamorous cell.

The black iron gates of his own abode eased open and the limo came to a stop in the circular driveway of the two-story mansion. An elegant structure of cream-colored stone, the house stood out even among the many jewels in the development. For him and Nadine, it didn't just say *we made it*, it was a place they'd envisioned living for many years and raising a large family.

Joachim preceded them into the house with the bags, and as soon as they entered, Philippa, the housekeeper, came shuffling into the large foyer. Her rotund face exploded into a big smile when she saw Antonella and Nadine.

"*¿Cómo estás, la chiquita?*" Philippa spread her arms wide, and Antonella ran into them, pressing her face into the woman's large bosom.

After their effusive greeting, she sent a more cautious smile in Nadine's direction. "*Hola, señora.* I have prepared the room next to Antonella for you."

"Thank you, Philippa." Nadine took the housekeeper's

hand. They had a special bond. Nadine had hired her, and when Cortez went on the road for months, the two had become very close. "I'm a little tired, so I think I'd like to take a nap, if that's okay." She turned to face Cortez.

Her eyes were so dark they appeared as shiny and luxurious as black onyx, and he was struck again by her effortless beauty. The brick-red top showed off the sepia-brown tone of her skin, and the straight bob cut framed her features perfectly—a round face, full nose, and a tasty mouth that could set his blood afire with the lightest brush.

He mentally shook himself when he realized they all awaited a response from him. "I think you both should probably get some rest after such a long flight." He looked pointedly at Antonella.

"We've been up since the crack of dawn," Antonella announced.

They all chuckled.

"On that note, we'll head up," Nadine said.

Antonella raced up the stairs, and Nadine followed behind at a more reasonable pace.

Philippa watched them go, hands clasped together in front of her. "It's good to have Mrs. Alesini back." She looked very pleased, smiling much more than the occasion warranted, as if Nadine was back for good.

"She's only here for a week," Cortez reminded her. Antonella's winter break ended next week.

"Yes, but it's a good way to start the New Year, isn't it?" Expectant brown eyes sought out his.

"It is," Cortez agreed in a measured voice. He dared not get too excited.

By the pleased expression on Philippa's face, his

answer sufficed. "I'll prepare dinner so that everyone can eat together."

"I won't be here for dinner." Cortez fished in his pocket for the keys to one of his cars. "I have an unplanned dinner meeting tonight—some business I need to wrap up before the wedding."

"Yes, sir." Philippa took off toward the kitchen.

She had been devastated when he and Nadine divorced, but not only for the dissolution of the marriage. She had come to love Antonella as one of her own. While she was accustomed to seeing his siblings and their families around, he lived alone in this house—a house she'd stated only a few months ago should be shared with a wife and children. Perhaps she felt sorry for him, but he had to dispel any wishful thoughts she had.

"Philippa."

"Yes, Mr. Alesini."

"Don't get your hopes up."

Her face shifted into a neutral expression. With a curt nod, she said, "Yes, sir."

Deep in thought, Cortez went into the garage. He climbed into the black Mercedes-Benz and drove through the gate. A quick glance at the clock on the dashboard let him know he had plenty of time before his dinner meeting at nine. Perfect, since he had to stop at the office to pick up and review several documents beforehand.

Tonight's meeting had been one he'd tried to avoid, but he was knee-deep in contract negotiations with the management team of a hot new boy band one of his scouts had seen playing at a riverside cafe in the Puerto Madero neighborhood. His record label, Musica Fuerte, wanted to sign them, but the boys' team of three—made up of two of the boys' parents who happened to be attorneys—was playing hardball. They knew the bankability of the young men. They were at the right age, ranging from fifteen to seventeen, good-looking, all played instruments, and sang in both Spanish and English.

The potential to make them into megastars was evident. He envisioned them becoming very popular in Latin America and even having crossover success in the United States, something he himself had only achieved on a small scale. *If* he could get their parents to adjust their unrealistic demands.

Cortez cruised to a stop behind several cars at the traffic light.

The outdoor cafés were filled with patrons sipping coffees, tea, reading, and chatting with friends. It reminded him of another time—the day he'd met Nadine. After their initial meeting, they'd had a whirlwind romance. Her family had warned her about her unemployed foreign boyfriend and his seductive conversation, but she'd ignored them all, as completely enamored with him as he had been with her.

Cortez gripped the steering wheel and accelerated behind the advancing traffic. Sentimentality threatened to overtake him, and much as he tried, he couldn't shake off the memories.

Her bottom may be a little fuller, her hips a little wider, but in essence, Nadine was the same woman he'd met fifteen years ago at that café—long before his singing career catapulted him to international stardom. At that first meeting, she'd made more than a great first impression on him.

He'd fallen in love with her.

CHAPTER 3

Fifteen years ago

Again and again, Cortez's eyes drifted to the young woman seated two tables over. She was hard to miss. Her thick hair was twisted into chunky plaits that she'd secured at her nape in a huge ball. Her skin stood out in stark contrast to the fairer-skinned people surrounding them, and unlike everyone else, including him, she sat alone, head bent over a book that had claimed her attention for the better part of thirty minutes.

Beside him, his lunch companion chuckled softly. Blond, with a winsome smile in a slightly pudgy face, Alec Rasmussen had become a close friend not long after he and Cortez met at a club a few years ago.

"Why don't you go talk to her?" Alec asked.

Cortez crumpled a napkin in his hand and tossed it onto the table. "What's the point? She's probably only here for a short time."

"Even better. Then you could have a fling and be done with it. No different than the others."

Ever since Alec's divorce had become final, he'd made sure to sleep with as many women as possible. He claimed to no longer believe in love and never wanted to get married again. He hung out in clubs with Cortez and his band, Los Tigres, which allowed him to indulge in the same women who flocked the stage whenever they performed.

"Maybe," Cortez murmured. But somehow he knew that wasn't true. This woman *was* different. She had an air about her. Something indefinable that had drawn his attention from the moment he spotted her.

She flipped a page in her book and happened to look up at him. Noticing him for the first time, she smiled—an expression so unguarded in its friendliness, he felt as if someone had jabbed him in the stomach with drumsticks. He was so shaken, he didn't realize he hadn't smiled back until she frowned and returned her gaze to the pages in front of her.

He had to get to know her.

Without a word to Alec, Cortez stood on legs that barely supported his weight. He'd never before experienced this type of reaction to a complete stranger. In fact, he was accustomed to women being overwhelmed by *his* presence, simply because he was a musician.

Standing on stage, sweat pouring down his face, strumming the guitar as he pelted out the latest tune he'd written, the screaming, jostling bodies offered encouragement on the road to fulfilling his dream of being a recording artist. For the first time, he understood the adoration he often received and almost laughed at the thought that for a change, he was the one weak-kneed.

Cortez walked over to her and stood beside the table, waiting for the young woman to look up again. When she did, her eyes filled with question.

"*Buenas tardes,*" she said, in a voice that brushed over him with the sensuality of soft silk and elicited shivers on his skin.

Shivers. He actually felt shivers at the sound of her voice.

"*¿Puedo ayudarte?*" she asked.

Cortez swallowed. Even with the distraction of unstable knees and goose-pimpled skin, he managed to pick up on the fact that she was indeed a foreigner. By her accent, an Anglophone. Perhaps from the United States.

"Yes, you can help me. Do you mind if I join you?" He gestured at the empty seat, holding his breath as he awaited her response.

She hesitated at first, her dark eyes flicking over the rest of the diners before returning to him. "No, I don't mind."

He breathed and sat down, giving her the smile he had forgotten earlier. "Pardon me for being so forward, but I couldn't help but notice you while I was sitting with my friend."

She didn't reply, but a faint, pleased smile lifted the corners of her lips. He wondered if they were as soft as they looked. Pillowy and full, they captured his attention for a moment as he imagined sucking her lower lip into his mouth and gently nipping it with his teeth.

She wasn't unfriendly, so he relaxed and leaned forward on one forearm. "Where are you from?"

"Atlanta."

"In Georgia?"

She giggled. "Yes."

"Why do you laugh?"

"Geor-gee-ah. I like the way you said it."

"Ah, you're making fun of my accent." He filled his voice with fake hurt.

Her eyes widened. "No, not at all. My Spanish pronunciation is really no good, so I'm not one to judge. It's just cute the way you said it."

"Cute?"

"Yes." She bit her bottom lip, perhaps a little embarrassed, or perhaps flirting with him. Either way, he was intrigued.

"How do you say it?" he asked.

"Georgia."

"Geor-juh," he repeated, mimicking her accent. "I like my way better."

"Oh really?" Her entire face smiled—her eyes, her lips, her skin. He had an overwhelming desire to keep that expression on her face.

"What brings you to Buenos Aires?"

"I work for an import/export consulting firm out of Atlanta. We offer advice and training for small businesses in Georgia that want to get involved in international trade." She spoke slowly, cautiously, still feeling him out. "They sent me here to work with a supplier and to get a better grasp on the language."

"A career woman."

"Something like that," she said.

Despite having local notoriety, for the time being, he only made a modest living as a musician. Los Tigres often performed for free in exchange for exposure and publicity. A woman like her might not be too interested in a man without stable employment. That didn't mean he couldn't try, though. All kinds of women were attracted to musicians—doctors, teachers, and corporate executives. And hopefully, an import/export consultant from Atlanta.

He never took his eyes from her face, giving her his undivided attention. It was a ploy he'd used in the past to get women, but this time he was genuinely interested in everything about her. "How long will you be in Argentina?"

"Five more months."

"You'll practically be a native when you leave. You'll have time to experience our culture, our food, our people."

"In between working," she said pointedly.

"Of course. Allow me to introduce myself. My name is Cortez Alesini. What is your name?" He extended his hand.

"Nadine…" She trailed off without giving her last name.

They shook hands, and when she tried to pull away, he held on for a fraction too long before allowing her to withdraw.

He didn't push. There would be ample time for that later. "How do you spell your name?"

"N-A-D-I-N-E."

He pretended to give the name some consideration, playfully stroking his jaw. "I would say Nah-deen," he said.

She shrugged. "Your pronunciation is different, but not so bad."

"I will call you whatever you wish from now on," he said, lowering his voice.

Her eyes widened at his impertinence. "From now on? Mr. Alesini—"

"Please, call me Cortez."

"Cortez."

Shivers anew when she said his name. All up and down his spine. "Yes?" he said politely, though his imagination had started to run wild with impolite thoughts. Like how would his name sound on her lips when she breathed it in his ear? Taut and damp beneath him, shivering as her fingers dug into his back? He couldn't wait to find out.

"What makes you think you'll have future opportunities to say my name?" She sounded mildly defiant, and the challenge in her eyes sparked determination in him.

He sat back in the chair, considering the best way to answer the question without scaring her off. Choosing to be forthright, he said, "We will be spending a lot of time together, Nadine."

"Is that so?" She clasped her hands on the table, punctuating the sarcastic question with a raised brow.

"Yes," he confirmed. "A lot of time."

Then he smiled. It was irrelevant to him whether or not she believed him, because he decided right then and there he was going to marry Nadine with no last name.

And he would give her his.

CHAPTER 4

"*N*adine, I am so sorry!"

Elsa sounded genuinely distraught on the phone, but Nadine didn't want to belabor the point about the lack of communication regarding the accommodations. Staying here meant she could spend more time with her daughter. Besides, her former sister-in-law had a full house over there, and even though it was after midnight, by the sound of the loud music and voices in the background, they had no intention of going to bed anytime soon. Staying at the mansion meant she had a better shot of keeping her sanity.

As the youngest of the Alesini children, Elsa was last to get married and a bit spoiled. At thirty-one, she was by no means a baby, but being twelve years younger than Cortez and fifteen years younger than Gustavo—the oldest—meant her older brothers often treated her more like a daughter than a sibling. Lucky for her, she would continue to be spoiled by her future husband, the wealthy son of a metals exporter.

"Don't worry about it, Elsa. It's fine. It's not as if Cortez and I can't get along."

"You are not angry, then?" the younger woman asked cautiously.

"Of course not. I know you're busy with the wedding preparations, and that's what you need to concentrate on."

"*Ay*, there is so much to do. Thank you for understanding. You are my sister, and I want you to be comfortable."

"I *am* comfortable. Don't concern yourself with me and my needs. What about you? Do you need me to do anything?"

"No, Mamá is here, my friends, and I am—" She broke off, her voice breaking. "I am so happy. Only two more days."

Nadine smiled, recalling how overwhelmed she'd been around the time of her own wedding, marrying a man in a foreign country and giving up her job to stay and make a life with him. Her friends and family had thought she was crazy, but she'd been high on love—a love stronger than the most potent of drugs.

She and Cortez didn't have much money at the time, so the wedding ceremony had taken place at Gustavo's *estancia*, a 200-acre ranch three hours outside of the city. With the mountains as a backdrop against the setting sun, she and Cortez said their vows in front of his entire family, her new friends, and the only members of her family able to attend—her parents.

"If you need me, you know you can call me."

"I will. See you Saturday!"

The call disconnected and Nadine sat on the side of the bed for a minute. It was strange to be back in this house as a guest when she knew every corner and cubby-hole and had been instrumental in designing much of the space. She'd selected linens for the beds, drapes for every window, and chosen furnishings shipped from abroad because they fit the specific décor of a room.

Pushing up from the bed at the grumbling in her stomach, she knew she had to eat something, even if only a snack. She quickly washed her face and brushed her teeth, then glanced down at her attire.

She hadn't brought a robe since she'd expected to be staying with Elsa, but the comfy shorts and tank top she slept in were decent enough to wear walking around the house. There wasn't much chance of anyone roaming through the halls at this hour anyway.

Closing the bedroom door as quietly as she could, Nadine tiptoed to the room next door. Easing open the door, she peeked in on her daughter, sleeping fitfully on the bed, before easing it shut again without a sound.

She crept down the stairs, stopping on the bottom step when she heard a sound, or thought she did. Tilting her head, she listened for movement or voices in other parts of the house, but heard nothing.

Finding her way in the dimness, she padded barefoot across the cool travertine tile that filled the open foyer, silently cursing herself for forgetting her bedroom slippers. At the back of the house, she fumbled for the electronic panel on the wall and illuminated the spacious kitchen.

Squinting, she waited until her eyes adjusted to the bright light before making her way to the French door refrigerator, a monstrosity of steel and glass that Cortez had insisted they buy, the one concession she and

Philippa allowed him when they had worked on designing the kitchen.

Nadine perused the shelves through the glass door, stacked with containers full of leftovers from the dinner Philippa had prepared. Before she indulged, she wanted something to drink.

She reached up and grasped a glass in the cabinet, and at the same moment, the hairs on her arms shot straight up. Immediately on alert, she swung around to find Cortez standing at the door.

He always moved so quietly and used to sneak up on her and steal a kiss or grab her around the waist and sweep her off the floor. Perhaps that's why she'd developed such an uncanny ability to detect whenever he was nearby.

"Find everything you need?" he asked.

"Yes. I was thirsty. Getting something to drink." She held up the glass as proof, but her hand trembled slightly, and she set it on the counter, suddenly nervous. Immensely uneasy.

"I'm thirsty, too," he said, coming toward her.

She stood there, immobile, unable to budge an inch as he neared, even when he reached up to the shelf behind her. The subtle scent of his skin swept below her nostrils, and she bit down on the inside of her cheek, grasping the counter behind her and not letting go until he'd moved away.

He appeared perfectly calm as he pulled a bottle of water from the refrigerator and poured himself a glass. She, on the other hand, had to force her breathing to return to normal.

Cortez tipped his head back and swallowed the water

in what seemed like only a couple of gulps, his Adam's apple bobbing up and down as the liquid swept down his throat. He'd made something so simple as drinking water appear manly and sexy.

He held out the bottle. "Would you like some?"

"Yes." Her throat was rather dry.

He filled the glass and she gladly swallowed a mouthful, wetting her parched throat.

Against her will, her gaze traveled down over his torso. She tried not to look, but his firm body was right there. She only had to stretch out a hand and she could touch the cluster of dark hairs on his chest, dragging her fingers through them to where they narrowed down into a thin column and disappeared below the waistband of his black silk pajama bottoms.

"Like what you see?"

Her eyes snapped up. The heat of mortification burned her cheeks. "I'm sorry. I—"

"Don't apologize." A muscle in his jaw tensed, the way it did when he reined in deep emotion. He set the bottle back in the refrigerator. "I have to admit, I do find it odd, though, that you would look at me like that."

"I don't know what you think you saw, but I assure you it was your imagination," Nadine said stiffly.

His eyes slid to her. "Yet you were about to apologize."

Once again, her cheeks burned hot. "I could accuse you of the same thing. You practically gave me a physical this afternoon."

"I'm not the one in a relationship."

"I'm not in a relationship."

"No? What about the man you're seeing?" He set his glass in the sink.

"Who are you talking about?" Nadine asked, genuinely confused.

"The doctor," he bit out.

"Clark?"

His shoulders drew taut as tightened guitar strings. "Is that his name?"

Cortez obviously knew much more than he let on, which made her wonder how he knew about her friend in the first place. Their conversations centered around Antonella, and every now and again he caught her up on news about one of their mutual friends, but they never discussed their paramours. Though she wasn't even sure Clark could be classified as one.

For years she feared jumping back into the dating pool, searching for a connection like the one she and Cortez had shared. Then a few months ago she met Clark, a single father whose boys attended the same Catholic school as Antonella.

A mere look from her ex and she melted, but that didn't happen with Clark. Unfortunately, the man bored her to tears. On the excitement barometer, it was like going from a superstar concert to a middle school talent show. After a few dates, they realized they were better off as friends.

"There's nothing going on between us. Not that I care what you think." She set her water on the counter and stalked toward the door, seeking escape, but his next words halted her in her tracks.

"You'd better care what I think," he said, voice low and lethal. "You will *not* bring another man into the house that *I* pay for."

Nadine rounded on him. "You think because you pay

for that house you own everything inside it?" Her eyes narrowed on him. "How did you even know about Clark? Are you grilling our daughter to get information about me and my personal affairs?"

A faint blush darkened his cheeks.

"That's despicable," she said.

His face tightened in anger. "What's despicable is having that man around our daughter."

"I have a right to date. We're no longer married." She held up her left hand so he could see her bare fingers.

Wrong thing to do. Seething anger entered his eyes, but still he maintained his cool—a trait that used to make steam blow from her ears when they were married. She wanted to see some emotion from him, to know what he was feeling.

"You'd better go to bed now," he said in a calm voice.

"Why?" she demanded. "Because you don't want to talk? That's so familiar. You always did an excellent job of avoiding conversation when we were married, traveling around, using your tour schedule as an excuse to stay away when you didn't want to deal with...the problems in our marriage."

She shut down as pain erupted inside of her, the kind that had kept her bedridden from depression, closed off from everyone around her until she found the strength to go on.

"I didn't need an excuse to stay away. My wife made it very clear I was not welcome in my own house." He tilted his head sideways. "Although...you never failed to welcome me in other ways."

A flash of heat swept Nadine's skin.

They'd never had any problems communicating in the

bedroom, driven by a sexual compulsion that surmounted their marital problems, though it couldn't make them disappear. After weeks on the road, the impatience with which he'd reach for her never failed to thrill her. So many times he'd tugged on her clothes, on more than one occasion tearing them from her body like a man possessed.

Every single time she'd matched his hunger, and her neck burned at the thought of him pushing her down into the bed, grabbing her thighs, pushing into her with the same focus, the same concentration he reserved for the craft of music.

"Does he know?" Cortez asked.

"Know what?" Nadine swallowed hard. She had to get out of there. She couldn't think straight.

"Does your boyfriend have any idea how insatiable you are?"

"He's not my boyfriend."

"Does he know how demanding you are? That when we were married, you required two, sometimes three orgasms in one night? That sometimes you wanted my tongue, and other times all you wanted was my rock hard c—"

Nadine swung at him, but he caught her wrist. His fingers tightened around her arm and she winced.

"That's not very nice. You should never resort to violence." He hauled her forward and she lost her balance, tumbling into his chest. She put out a hand to brace herself and the springy hairs tickled her palm.

"All right, you've proved your point," Nadine said in a tremulous whisper.

"No." His gray-blue eyes scoured her face. He examined her features as though branding her image into his brain. Below his waist, she could feel his body stir to life. "I haven't proven my point yet."

Then he crushed her mouth beneath his.

CHAPTER 5

They'd been edging toward this explosive kiss from the minute they started arguing—maybe even from the moment they saw each other at the airport.

Cortez's tongue pressed against the seam of her mouth, and with embarrassing ease, Nadine's lips fell apart to allow the moist invasion. He swept the interior with such boldness, such authority, that a tremor rattled through her body. The kiss consumed and took over all her senses. Explosive. Powerful. Like a pyrotechnic display with no holds barred.

Cortez cradled the back of her head in his large hand and sifted his fingers through her short hair, keeping her locked against him. Her scalp tingled at his touch, and her heart careened against her ribs in excitement. It had been so long since she'd felt his hands on her and his mouth on hers. She strained to get closer, eagerly sucking and gorging on the sweetness of his flavor.

His hand climbed up her side beneath her shirt and her breasts drew tight and throbbed, demanding to be touched. When he finally covered one with his warm hand, she released a low, heavy moan of immense relief and tipped her head back. His mouth immediately fastened on her neck, tongue tracing the arch of her throat while his hand squeezed her breast and she trembled, overwhelmed by sensation as her nipple swelled against his cupping hand.

She noted that the texture of his hand had softened. Rough calluses, from years of playing music, were gone from the tips of his broad fingers. His other hand pushed beneath the hem of her loose shorts and grabbed one butt cheek. Deep in a sensual haze, Nadine arched her hips, grinding against the thick arousal tenting his pants to relieve the swelling ache between her thighs. It was as if they'd leaped back in time—pawing, grabbing, kissing on each other with unchecked enthusiasm.

Suddenly, Cortez lifted his head and looked down at Nadine with half-closed eyes that glittered with need, his heavy breathing ragged and unstable. "Now I've proven my point," he rasped.

His warm breath brushed against her lips, and the thumb stroking along the crease of her hip wreaked havoc with her nerves. With an abrupt shake of the head, he released her, staring at her in wide-eyed disbelief, obviously shaken by the powerful attraction that still existed between them.

Nadine staggered back and grabbed onto the butcher-block island at her back for balance. She needed to put distance between them, but for the moment couldn't move—could barely even think. Her brain had shut down.

She didn't know what had made him stop, but she was glad one of them had done so. If it had been up to her, they'd be horizontal on the kitchen floor in a few minutes. Something they'd done before. In fact, they'd christened almost every nook of the house, and she was hard-pressed to find a room in which he hadn't made her come.

When he touched her like that, she could almost forget why they'd divorced. Strangers, virtual enemies in the end, they used to square off like boxers, retreating to their own corners after they'd lobbed verbal blows at each other that bruised egos and hurt feelings.

The loudest noise in the room was the trembling inhalation of her breaths. She couldn't control the sound, a glaring manifestation of how undone she'd become by a simple kiss. Yet nothing was simple with Cortez. She couldn't believe that after three years she still reacted so strongly to him.

"You had no right to do that." Her voice was unsteady. She took a deep breath. "Tomorrow I'm getting a hotel."

"You will not stay in a hotel," Cortez said between gritted teeth.

"Well, I can't stay here if you're going to maul me," Nadine shot back, completely ignoring her own role in their heated kiss. She held a hand to her lips to hide their trembling.

"You're an Alesini," he said, as if that explained everything.

"In name only. You're not responsible for me."

"You're the mother of my child! I will always be responsible for you, and you will not stay in a hotel like a stranger." The vehemence in his voice took her by surprise. She didn't know what upset him more. The denial of his name or the desire to find lodging elsewhere.

"Of course Antonella would rather have you here," he

added in a calmer voice. "Stay. I...won't touch you again." He clenched his hands into fists.

Nadine swallowed. "How do I know I can trust you?"

"Don't raise your hand to me and you have nothing to worry about," Cortez said in a raw tone.

She angled her chin upward but watched him warily, doubting him.

"You have my word. I promise to keep my hands to myself. I had a momentary lapse in judgment and it won't happen again."

"If you touch me again, I'm leaving," Nadine warned.

Tension hummed in the room as they stared at each other. She waited for his response, but when there was none forthcoming, she found the strength to leave. Hurrying from the room, she raced up the stairs on unsteady legs, managing on adrenaline alone. When she shut the door to the bedroom, she couldn't make it to the bed. It might as well have been a thousand miles away.

She was shaking so badly, she slid to the floor. He'd branded her in multiple ways. She touched her fingers to her lips. They burned from the heat of his kiss, and the taste of him remained on her tongue. Even his scent—masculine, robust—had been absorbed into her skin.

In no time at all, Cortez had made her feel jittery and out of control. As if their years apart had never been, and no time had passed at all.

She still had seven days to go.

* * *

RAKING A HAND THROUGH HIS HAIR, a line of bitter curses flew from Cortez's lips.

He waited until he thought Nadine was back in her bedroom before he risked taking the stairs. His body tightened as he passed her bedroom door, and he almost pushed his way in to relieve the lust raging through his body.

He was forty-three years old, but she had him as discombobulated as a man with far less maturity. The thick pounding of blood in his veins had shot south within moments, turning his flesh hard and unyielding, hungry for a chance to bury deep inside of her. He knew he should exercise some measure of self-control, but Nadine made him feel out of control. Always had. She elicited emotional responses from him that no one else could. He'd written songs about life, the birth of their daughter, and his family, but it was Nadine who had inspired his best work.

She'd been there less than twenty-four hours—less than *twelve* hours—and he hadn't been able to resist touching her. If he couldn't go twelve hours, how the hell was he going to make it through the next week?

Cortez banked the corner and pushed open the double doors of the master bedroom suite. In the silent room, he lay on his back and placed a hand over his groin and his hefty erection. He massaged his stiff flesh through the silk pants, but it wasn't enough. He grimaced as sexual hunger continued to run rampant through him.

Closing his eyes, he slipped a hand beneath the waistband and stroked his hard erection. Then he let his imagination run wild with everything he wanted to do to his wife.

Ex-wife.

CHAPTER 6

*N*adine woke up to pallid light streaming through the sheer curtains and the muffled sounds of mowers cutting the grass outside. She stretched, feeling somewhat rested. At some point her mind had settled enough to fall asleep, but not before she'd tortured herself with thoughts of Cortez and wondered if she had, indeed, made a mistake by agreeing to stay in the house with him.

At a short rap on the door, she twisted her head and Antonella traipsed into the room wearing a pair of capris and a T-shirt. Her loose hair tumbled down the middle of her back, and her bright, happy face made Nadine smile.

Antonella hopped onto the bed with a lot of energy, looking like she'd been up for hours, which was probably the case. Like her father, she didn't need much sleep. As long as Cortez could catch a refreshing nap every now and again, he could go for long periods without extended rest.

"What are we doing today?" her daughter asked.

Nadine twirled a lock of Antonella's hair around her finger and yawned. "I need breakfast first, but just because I'm here, don't think you can't do what you normally do when you come to see your dad. You don't have to keep me company."

She tweaked Antonella's nose and then rolled out of bed. She went into the en suite bathroom, a sleekly designed space in timeless black and white. Her fingers briefly touched the pewter-framed mirror, a piece she and the decorator had both seen at the same time and simultaneously cried, "That one!"

She smiled a little to herself. That day was a long time ago.

"I might watch a movie in the theater. Or go down the street to one of my friends—Kara's house. I don't think she knows I'm back yet." Katarina was the daughter of a couple who owned a chain of clothing stores.

"If you go down the street, let Joachim walk with you. Or I'll take you." Nadine peeked out the door at Antonella, who was plucking at the sheet. "Understand?"

Her daughter's head popped up. "Yes."

"You don't walk around here by yourself, do you?" One couldn't be too careful, even in a neighborhood like this.

"No," Antonella said in a small voice, lowering her eyes, which made Nadine suspect it was an untruth. She'd address that issue with Cortez later.

"Did you eat breakfast?" She started brushing her teeth.

"Yep." Antonella came to stand in the doorway, a mischievous look on her face. "Since you were so late,

Papá and I ate all the *medialunas*. Nothing's left. Not a single crumb." She licked her lips for good measure.

Medialunas were small, crescent-shaped pastries that looked like miniature croissants, but had a sweeter taste. They were part of a typical Argentine breakfast, and Nadine loved to sweeten hers even more by cutting open the flaky bread and swiping on a healthy serving of *dulce de leche*. She'd learned that from Cortez, who had a sweet tooth like she did, and something their daughter had inherited from both of them.

Nadine finished up at the sink. "Nah-uh. You better not have."

"Uh-huh. And I'm not sorry."

"Oh yeah?"

Nadine darted after her daughter, and Antonella took off running with a loud screech. When Nadine caught her, she tackled her onto the bed and tickled her mercilessly.

"This is your punishment for being so mean to your mother."

Antonella squealed and laughed, wriggling and twisting to get away from Nadine's poking fingers.

"Are you sorry?" Nadine asked, continuing to dig and prod while holding her so she couldn't escape.

"Yes. I'm...sorry," Antonella choked out. "We...didn't eat them...all."

"That's what I thought. You know better." Nadine released Antonella, and her daughter brushed away her thick hair, which had tumbled into her face during their playful tussle.

Nadine looked down into her daughter's dark eyes, her heart hurting a little as it filled with emotion. Her baby, her one and only. "You know I love you," she said softly.

Antonella nodded, her face grave. "More than life itself."

She'd told her that a thousand times. Squeezing her daughter tight, she pressed a long, loud kiss to her cheek. If anything happened to her…She cast aside the devastating thought, one that was too unbearable in its familiarity.

She retrieved her suitcase and dropped it onto the bed. "I guess I better get dressed and have some breakfast. Your *tío* Gustavo and his family will be here soon."

"I can't wait to see Gabriela," Antonella said, her eyes lighting up.

Gabriela was Gustavo's daughter, only a year older than Antonella, and her favorite cousin. Gustavo had six children in all, five boys and Gabriela. When they arrived, the house would be alive with activity.

* * *

NADINE CHANGED and had breakfast on the back terrace overlooking the lake. On the opposite side, a father and son fed the ducks, who squawked loudly as they chased after the morsels of bread. This side featured a dock where a small row boat was moored, and a shallow beach where they used to sit and roast marshmallows or relax under the stars with blankets and a small fire, a tradition she knew Cortez continued when Antonella came to visit.

She hadn't seen Cortez this morning yet, and that was a good thing. It gave her a chance to put on her mask and secure her defenses in place.

According to her daughter, he went to his home office after breakfast. He still had details from a deal to work out, which he wanted to have completed so he could spend quality time with Antonella during the rest of her stay.

She and her daughter went to the home theater. Instead of sitting in the tall-back leather seats, they sat in the overstuffed sofa that ran along the rear wall. It was filled with giant pillows, and was a comfy alternative to the chairs. Antonella stretched out beside Nadine for a Harry Potter marathon.

Late morning and halfway through the first movie, Nadine's former in-laws arrived, sooner than expected. Philippa came to announce their arrival, and that's when all the commotion started. Antonella rushed out and Nadine followed her. By the time she made it outside, Antonella and Gabriela had already fallen into each other's arms with gleeful squeals.

Cortez stood outside in jeans and a ribbed gray shirt, his handsome face brightened with joy, greeting his much taller and huskier brother, Gustavo, beside a gray SUV. His wife, Gabriela, three of the boys, and their luggage, arrived in that vehicle, while his eldest, Carlos, had driven behind in a blue sedan with the second oldest.

Gustavo was a giant of a man at six foot five, with beefy arms and a weather-worn face that came from working out in the elements. His stern features belied a gentle nature, and his black hair was streaked with more gray than Cortez's. By contrast, his wife, Benita, was a petite woman with reddish-blonde hair, a soothing smile, and a very pregnant belly—baby number seven.

There were hugs and kisses all around, and finally

Benita stopped to beam at Nadine. "It's so good to see you."

"Good to see you, too. Boy or girl this time?" Nadine asked.

"*Gracias a Dios*, a girl this time. No more boys." She giggled and rubbed her belly.

Carlos, almost as tall as his father but with a slighter build, pulled a cooler from the trunk of the blue sedan he arrived in. From a quick check, Nadine saw the vehicle contained more coolers, and she knew plenty of meat and food had been brought.

That could only mean one thing. They were going to have a party.

CHAPTER 7

K *eep your distance.*

That's what Cortez kept telling himself, and it was easier to do with a house abuzz with activity. He welcomed the revelry of his cousins and friends, who'd arrived after Gustavo put out the call for the party. Cortez sat just on the outskirts, watching the festivities from his vantage point on the patio, lanterns positioned around the heart-shaped pool adding enough light to see, but keeping the atmosphere cozy.

Gustavo had brought plenty of fresh meat from his ranch and the men had spent the afternoon grilling steaks, chicken, and chorizo. Side dishes of salad, potatoes, rice, and empanadas had been delivered in chafing dishes from a local restaurant. Joachim had made two trips to the wine cellar for bottles of Malbec, and a separate trip to the store for beer and other spirits. Philippa and two of the maids had set up the food and tables around the pool, while Benita and Nadine worked in the kitchen preparing chimichurri to accompany the steaks.

Now that the party was in full swing, everyone was having a good time—talking, eating, and some even dancing. The kids occupied themselves away from the adults. Antonella and Gabriela had discovered the gelato in the deep freezer, so they and the other children bulldozed through the inventory eating the frozen treat while huddled in a big group at one end of the pool.

Gustavo staggered over, bottle of beer in hand, and plopped down onto the chair next to Cortez. He was already drunk, and when his brother drank, he talked a lot. Cortez braced for the coming conversation.

"She looks great." He directed his gaze over to Nadine, standing with his wife on the other side of the pool. "How do you plan to get her back?"

"I don't." He sipped his wine. The rich flavor washed over his tongue, but not even the exquisite taste of the grape could compare to the sweetness he'd sampled when he'd kissed Nadine last night.

Gustavo frowned. "What do you mean? Why is she here at the house with you, then?"

Cortez explained the mix-up with Elsa.

With an overly hearty laugh that shook his large frame, Gustavo tossed his head back. Definitely drunk.

"And you believe her?" He snorted. "Our little sister is playing matchmaker. She wants the two of you back together."

The same thought had crossed his mind, but Cortez had dismissed it; because if it was true, he'd have to throttle Elsa—thereby leaving her fiancé without a bride.

"You loved each other once," Gustavo said, speaking in a grave voice like a wise man imparting knowledge from years of experience. "Benita and I don't always get along.

41

Our parents don't always get along. Marriage is work, and you don't give up because of a rough patch." He tossed back a swallow of beer.

"We didn't give up." Everyone tried to break down their split into simplistic terms. Give up. Stop fighting. Nothing could be further from the truth. "Our situation is more complicated than that." He sipped his wine.

"Why? Because you couldn't have any more children?"

Cortez stiffened at the blunt question.

"You can have one of mine," his brother continued. He took a swig of beer, unaware in his inebriated state that he'd just torn open an old wound.

"I'd rather have my own," Cortez murmured.

Coming from large families—he with five brothers and sisters and Nadine with six—they'd both wanted a large family of their own. But after Antonella, getting pregnant had been difficult. For years they'd tried, and for years he watched her struggle to keep her hopes up. Being around his family didn't help. Every year at least one of his siblings welcomed a new baby into the world, and their family celebrated. Every year, he and she waited, and hoped, and prayed they'd be able to celebrate, too.

After some time, he stopped talking about having children because he didn't want her to feel any pressure. Then the unthinkable happened, and she never quite recovered. Her vibrancy and optimism had been snuffed out, and he couldn't fix it. She became fifty percent alive and one hundred percent unhappy, and he was never able to put a genuine smile on her face again—something he'd promised himself he would always do. Keep her smiling. Keep her happy.

"You can have your own children," Gustavo said. "If

not with Nadine, then find another woman. You can have any woman you want."

But he only wanted one.

His eyes flicked over to Nadine, who stood swaying gently to the music as she and Benita spoke. She'd been with him from the beginning. He wanted her with him in the end.

* * *

NADINE MUNCHED on a delicious meat empanada, waiting for Benita to return from the bathroom.

She'd missed this. The welcoming nature of the Alesini clan had made her transition into the culture that much easier, but it hadn't been a completely smooth transition. A few relatives had questioned Cortez's decision to marry a woman who, in their words, didn't fit into their "homogenous" family structure, but he'd swiftly and firmly squashed such comments. If anyone else had a problem with her, she was not aware, and eventually her mind settled that her mixed race daughter would have no problem fitting in.

She watched as Cortez came toward her from the other side of the pool. They'd done an excellent job of avoiding each other for most of the day, but as he neared, her heart made a worrisome flutter in her chest.

He bestowed a lazy smile on her. "I bet you don't miss all this craziness," he said.

He was trying to be polite, pretending like last night hadn't happened. For the sake of appearances, she went along with him.

"Southern families can be just as crazy and boisterous."

"Hmm…" He looked down into his almost-empty glass of wine as if the answers to the mysteries of the universe were contained within. "I wouldn't know."

Just as members of his family had been skeptical about their union, members of hers had been as well. Their concerns had been rooted in the fact that her decision to abandon her home and job was based solely on falling in love—an emotion they doubted she actually felt. They thought her decision impulsive and imprudent, and worried about how Cortez would support her without a "real job."

"My parents didn't dislike you. They just…didn't understand how I could walk away from everything to move here."

"Even after we achieved all of this, they never fully accepted our marriage. They must be glad you're back home."

"They're not happy my marriage fell apart, if that's what you mean."

They both fell silent.

"Would you ever consider moving back?" He spoke even slower than usual, his words a bit slurred.

She eyed his glass. "How much have you had to drink?"

"Not as much as Gustavo."

"That's not saying much." He laughed, and she hazarded a grin. As big as Gustavo was, he was always the first to get drunk. Benita and Carlos would have quite a struggle getting him up the stairs to bed tonight.

"Would you move back?" Cortez pressed, his face inscrutable.

"You've had too much to drink."

"I'm not drunk." Emotion radiated from his eyes. "Answer the question."

"Don't do this." Her heart started racing.

"Do what?"

"You're trying to force an answer out of me."

"What are you afraid of?"

You.

"Was it so terrible?" he asked, softly. He lifted a hand, about to touch her cheek or her hair, so close that only a sliver of air separated them.

"I left, didn't I?"

The question stopped him mid-motion. His fingers crumbled into a fist and his face became shuttered.

Nadine turned away. "Didn't we hurt each other enough? Let's not do this."

He didn't respond right away. The beat of the music and the sounds of laughter and conversation around the patio filled her ears.

"You're right," he said tersely.

With the flick of a wrist, Cortez tossed his glass against the back wall. It shattered into a dozen pieces, and Nadine flinched, jarred by the manifestation of his anger. She remained rooted to the spot, watching his stiff back as he disappeared into the house.

Other than a few heads turned in their direction, no one else noticed what he'd done, or the remnants of wine sliding down the cream-colored brick like drops of blood.

CHAPTER 8

*W*hat a night. And they still had hours to go.

Stifling a yawn, Nadine dragged into the hotel ballroom on sore feet. She rolled her stiff neck and wiggled her shoulders to loosen the tight muscles. Some of the guests had left, but the wedding was still going strong. For the most part, an empty table meant the occupants were on the dance floor. Young, old, and in-between. She had no idea where they got the energy from.

At the moment, neither the bride nor groom could be seen for the throng of family and friends that surrounded them, dancing to a pop song played by the live band. The entire group gyrated and jumped around as if it wasn't almost six in the morning.

None of this was a surprise. Argentine weddings had a habit of starting at night and lasting into the next day, so Nadine had prepared by taking a nap beforehand. She'd still done good to last this long. Soon enough she'd be leaving, but she first had to lay eyes on her daughter.

Scanning the dim room, illuminated by candles on

each table and a ball casting flashes of light as it twirled from the ceiling, she didn't see Antonella anywhere. Knowing her twelve-year-old, she was probably in the middle of the madness with her family members.

Across the room, Cortez stood near a wall with a small plate in hand, talking to the wedding planner and one of the hotel employees. He'd long ago gotten rid of his tie and jacket like many of the men in the room, wearing only a white shirt and black trousers—two very basic colors that somehow managed to magnify his sex appeal.

Her eyes lingered on his bent head and profile, recalling his display of anger the night before. She and Cortez went together about as well as winter and summer, and they'd made sure to steer clear of each other as much as possible. Easy enough to do in a house of that size. While she relaxed poolside with Benita and the youngest boys, he spent time with Antonella and Gabriela at the park. While she napped, they watched movies or played air hockey in the game room. It was all very civilized.

Right then he looked up, and Nadine's stomach contracted. They'd arrived in the limo, which had been a painfully quiet ride, occasionally disrupted by Antonella and Gabriela snickering with their heads together, oblivious to the tension between her and Cortez.

Nadine sent him a brief smile, one that she hoped he saw as a peace offering. They had to do better than this. Gustavo and his family were leaving tomorrow, which meant she and Cortez would no longer have the buffer of family between them.

To her surprise, he smiled back, and she took a

relieved breath. With five more days left on this trip, it was better if they got along.

He said a few words to the hotel contact, nodded, and then walked in her direction. The closer he came, the more the air charged, and she wondered if he felt it, too. Or was she the only one who experienced the sizzle—the crackle around them whenever they were in the same vicinity?

Cortez swiveled a chair from a nearby table in the same direction as hers, so he could watch the dance floor as well. He dropped into it with a groan.

"Don't tell me you're tired," Nadine said.

"Okay, I won't tell you."

"This should be nothing for you. You used to put on a concert, party into the morning, and then stroll into a TV studio for a live interview."

Crossing an ankle over his knee, he said, "The good old days." He sliced into the hunk of cake on his plate. "Mmmm. *Delicioso.*"

Nadine eyed the dessert. "Is that the first piece you've had all night?"

Cortez nodded. "They set this aside for me." He shot her a look from the corner of his eye and arched a brow. "How many have you had?'

"Don't worry about how many I've had," she snapped.

The sexy smile he was known for appeared as he laughed quietly to himself. "Is that two or three slices?"

"What did I just say?" Nadine asked.

He full-on chuckled this time. Sliding his gaze to hers, he shook his head and said, "You truly haven't changed a bit."

Nadine shifted her gaze away from him to hide the reaction to his words, to his face, to his very presence.

"You can have mine." Cortez extended the plate to her.

"This is the last of it?" Nadine glanced toward the table where the delicious three-tier masterpiece covered in white fondant and filled with passionfruit custard had previously been displayed.

"No more," he confirmed.

She shook her head. "No, that's yours. I couldn't." Plus she'd already had two slices.

He shoved the plate closer, and the moist layers of the dessert called out to her. "I insist. I've had enough."

She sincerely doubted that. Her lust for sweets was legendary, but she found her match in him. "I can't possibly eat all of this alone. You'll have to share it with me."

"Deal." He scooted the chair closer.

In the past, she would have simply used Cortez's fork, but something as simple as that would be considered inappropriate now. Too intimate. She unrolled a cloth napkin and used the fork inside to cut off a slice of the cake. Slipping it into her mouth, she moaned with satisfaction.

"I want to kiss the baker," she murmured.

Cortez laughed at her right before placing a hunk of cake in his mouth.

She took off another piece, and they quietly went back and forth, eating the delicious dessert. It reminded her of other occasions, in the beginning when they had struggled as newlyweds and a night out meant sharing a meal and splitting dessert afterward. They *always* made sure they had enough money for dessert.

Anyone looking at them could easily mistake them for a couple from those years past, the way they shared the plate, held upright in his hand, cutting and eating and savoring each bite together.

When the last morsel remained, Cortez's gaze bounced from her to the plate and back to her again. "Go ahead," he said, with a slight nod.

Nadine shook her head. "It's the last piece, and it was yours originally, so you should have it."

"Take it."

He spoke quietly, and she knew he meant it. He might even become a little upset if she didn't take it.

The simple generosity made her blink back tears. With numb lips she said, "Thank you." Nothing but crumbs remained after she placed the last piece of cake in her mouth.

Chewing slowly, it took a while for Nadine to get it all down. When she did, she set the fork on the table beside her.

Then she turned and met her ex-husband's steady gaze.

"Are you happy in Atlanta?" His face was pensive and shuttered, hiding his emotions with the same effectiveness of someone lowering the shades on a window to block out all light.

Happy.

She'd thought she was—and on some level, she truly was. She had her health, a good job, and her daughter. After coming here, however, she felt more like someone who'd fooled herself into thinking she was happy—living a life that, little by little, was being exposed for the lie that it was.

The attraction between her and Cortez was undeniable, and it didn't take a genius to deduce that what she felt was more than attraction. So how could she ever truly be happy when the man she used to love—she swallowed the obvious lie—still loved, lived thousands of miles away?

Her eyes shifted toward the gyrating dancers. Cortez's parents had already left, but his aunt was on the floor, shimmying with her husband and giving the younger generation stiff competition.

"I'm—" she pushed the words past the knot in her throat, "—I'm as happy as I can be."

She didn't see his reaction, but when he responded in a low voice, she thought she heard him say, "That's all that matters."

"Are you?" she asked, keeping her eyes on the dance floor.

"As happy as I can be."

There were so many more questions she wanted to ask, but she was afraid of the answers.

Why did he let her go? Did he regret marrying her, since she couldn't give him the children he wanted? Or did he regret the divorce, dreading living without her the way she dreaded living without him—seeing the sobering truth of her life stretched before her like a vast, empty wasteland?

Servers began bringing out chafing dishes filled with food, which meant breakfast would be served shortly. This was her cue to leave, to escape this conversation that brought her more pain than she wanted to bear at the moment.

"I'm going to leave." She rose from the chair and he

stood, too.

"I'm going to stay for breakfast," he said.

She'd expected him to. "I'll say goodbye to Antonella and then catch a cab."

"Don't do that. I'll call Joachim and have him take you home." He reached into his pocket for his cell phone.

"I'm one person. If I take the car, what about you and Antonella and—"

"We'll be fine." He waved away her concern. "There are enough cars among us all that everyone can get home with no problem."

"It doesn't make sense—"

"Take the car, Nadine!"

Her head tipped back at his heated response.

"Just…take it."

"All right," she mumbled.

Without another word, she walked away from him and went in search of Antonella. She craned her neck and finally saw their daughter, dancing in the corner with Gabriela. Two of their male cousins danced with them.

Nadine wound her way across the room, stopping often to say goodbye to friends and former in-laws she wouldn't see again—perhaps ever, once they went back to their homes. She squeezed Elsa tight, whose bright smile hadn't dimmed since they entered the ballroom, and whispered words of encouragement, telling her how happy she was for her and her new husband. By the time she made it over to the children, her daughter had spotted her.

"You're leaving?" Antonella asked, pouting. Her hair had been tamed into a low chignon, held in place by a series of pearl-lined clips.

"It's late, and I'm going to get some sleep before the sun comes up. I'll see you later today."

"Okay."

Nadine gave her a tight squeeze and then slipped through the double doors toward the hotel exit. More tired than she'd realized, she dozed a little in the limo, but woke up when Joachim pulled into the driveway.

"See you later, Joachim," she called, as she walked toward the front door.

"*Hasta luego, señora,*" he called back. He waited until she'd let herself into the house before strolling off in the direction of the entrance to the servants' quarters.

Nadine undressed quickly and fell into bed, her head barely touching the pillow before she was asleep.

Sometime later, she jolted awake. At first she thought the sun had disturbed her rest, the way it slanted through the drapes covering the French doors that led to the balcony. But as her sleep-muddled brain became more aware of her surroundings, she realized the sound of someone pounding ceaselessly on the door had woken her up.

"*¡Señora, despiértate, por favor!*" The desperate voice of Philippa, the housekeeper, could be heard through the wooden partition.

Rubbing her eyes, Nadine sat up quickly. "Come in," she called.

Philippa burst in, her face crumpled in worry and hands clutching the telephone. Panic shot through Nadine's veins. A sixth sense told her that whatever was wrong had to do with her daughter.

"Señor Alesini is on the *teléfono.* You must to go now. There has been an accident. *La chiquita* is in the hospital!"

CHAPTER 9

Nadine tore out of the elevator and marched down the stark white hospital hallway toward the nurse's station. Her body shook with the type of fear that drowned out all other thoughts and feelings, focused on her sole goal, which was to get to her daughter. She couldn't breathe easy until she saw Antonella in one piece.

She was almost to the desk when she saw Cortez coming toward her. Stubble shadowed his unshaven chin and jaw, and his white shirt and black slacks were much more rumpled now.

Her eyes zeroed in on a dark smudge about the size of a quarter on the left side of his shirt, and her hand flew to her mouth. "Is that blood?" she asked in a terrified whisper.

"It is, but—"

"*What?*" The room started spinning. "Where is she? Where is she?"

"Nadine, calm down. Listen to me." Cortez reached for her, but she brushed aside his hands.

"I will not calm down. Tell me where she is. Tell me where my baby is!" She grabbed the lapels of his shirt.

He grasped her by the arms. "*Escúchame*. Listen to me." He spoke in a calm but firm voice. "She is fine. She is not seriously hurt. I tried to explain everything to you on the phone, but you hung up so fast."

"If she's not seriously hurt, then whose blood is that?" Nadine demanded in a whisper.

"It's hers, but—"

The hospital sounds became muffled, as if someone had placed noise-reducing headphones over her ears. Her knees went weak, and as if from a distance, she heard Cortez curse under his breath.

Fingers biting into her arms, he dragged her over to a group of chairs. "Sit," he said in a grim voice, pushing her down onto one of the seats. He sat down beside her and held onto one wrist, as if he feared she'd run off.

He waited as she took several deep breaths to stave off the fuzziness that had encroached on the perimeter of her brain.

"She's going to be okay." He continued to speak in a mild, low tone. "She has a bruise on her head and a broken wrist. It's a minor fracture, the doctor said, so they put a splint on it. I have blood on my shirt because when I pulled her from the car, shattered glass had nicked her skin and caused some bleeding."

"Where is she?"

"Room 2201, down the hall. They want to keep her for the rest of the day for observation because she bumped her head. It's just a precaution."

Nadine took a few more deep breaths, fighting back the clawing panic. Terrible things happened in hospitals.

Cortez's hand tightened around her wrist. "You have to calm down. She's already shaken, and if she sees you like this, it will upset her more."

She nodded her understanding. She had to be strong for her baby.

"Do you want some water?"

She shook her head, even though her mouth felt as dry as the Monte Desert in western Argentina. "No. I just want to see her."

Cortez took a deep breath. "All right. Let's go."

He rose from the chair and Nadine followed him, taking the time during the short walk to pull herself together. As he said, if she appeared distressed, it would only upset Antonella more.

"How are the other kids?" she asked.

Cortez paused outside the door. His eyes held concern as he looked down at her. "They're all fine and Gustavo took them to the house after they were checked out. You probably passed each other on the road."

Antonella had been riding with her cousins—Gabriela, her older brother, Carlos, and her second-oldest brother —when a vehicle sideswiped them. Even though Antonella was the most banged up of the car's occupants, Nadine was thankful that the injuries were not severe for anyone else in the car.

Cortez pushed open the door to room 2201, but let Nadine precede him. When she saw her daughter lying there beneath the white sheets, her pale face just a shade or two darker than the stark white pillowcase her head rested on, she almost fell apart.

She'd experienced this type of emotional turmoil before.

A child. A hospital. But that time the results had been disastrous. Devastating.

With the same determination that she'd exercised for years, Nadine slammed the door on the memory, forcing the image of tiny little fingers and toes from her mind. She treated that time the way she always had—as if it had never occurred.

"Mommy." Antonella lifted her arms and Nadine rushed to her side, dropping onto the firm mattress and gathering her in her arms.

"Are you okay, baby?" She petted her daughter's curly hair, which had fallen free of the clips that had held it in place.

"Yes," her daughter replied, voice muffled against her breast.

"Mommy's here now." She brushed hair from Antonella's forehead to get a good look at her and saw a mean-looking purple bump on her temple. "That looks pretty nasty." She touched it and her daughter winced.

"The nurse says I have to stay here."

"Only until the end of the day." Cortez walked over to the chair near the wall and sat down. Though he spoke in a reassuring voice, Nadine read the anxiety in his expression. His well-coiffed hair was no longer neat and tidy—probably pushed into all directions by fingers motivated by worry. He was unshaven, disheveled, and looked like he needed to sleep.

Their gazes connected over the top of Antonella's head. He didn't have to say a word. She read everything in his clear gray eyes. He and she weren't just two parents worried about the wellbeing of their child.

They were two parents who'd already experienced the tragedy of losing one.

CHAPTER 10

*N*adine closed the drapes on the windows in her daughter's bedroom, so in the morning the sun's rays wouldn't disturb her sleep. Then she moved quietly over the carpeted floor, making her way over to the bed where she slept.

She sighed, tucking the sheets around Antonella more securely.

At the hospital, Cortez had dismissed the notion that he needed to go home and get some rest. He'd spent the entire day there and taken a nap in the chair, which temporarily revived him. They'd eaten lunch and dinner in the room with Antonella, played games, read, and while she napped, they watched TV. Neither wanted to leave her alone, and they kept a close eye on her, right along with the medical personnel.

Though reluctant to let her out of her sight, Nadine finally dropped a featherlight kiss on her cheek and walked over to the door. When she opened it, Gabriela stood on the other side, eyes widening when she saw Nadine.

"Hi," the girl said in a low voice.

Nadine spoke to her in Spanish. "Why aren't you in bed?"

"I wanted to see Antonella. Can I stay in here tonight?" Gabriela asked timidly.

Cortez had moved another bed into Antonella's room so the girls could be close.

"Of course you can." She tilted up Gabriela's chin. "You're okay?"

Gabriela nodded vigorously.

Nadine smiled. "Go on." She stepped out of the way and Gabriela entered the bedroom and climbed into the other bed.

Nadine quietly shut the door and went downstairs to the kitchen. She found Cortez in there, standing in front of the butcher-block island, staring down into a glass of water with a deep frown on his face. He still hadn't changed out of his clothes.

He looked up when she came in.

"She's sleeping," Nadine said. "Gabriela's in the room with her now."

He rubbed a tired hand across his brow. "Gustavo asked if she could stay when they go home tomorrow. She wants to stay until Antonella leaves to go back to the States. I told him that it was fine."

"They're close. I know they like to spend as much time together as possible."

Nadine stepped further into the room and took a fortifying breath, bracing for the conversation to come, a conversation they hadn't been able to have at the hospital. "How did this happen? And by the way, I'm not judging."

His thin lips compressed into a narrow line. "Of course not."

"I just want to know how our daughter ended up in a car filled with a bunch of teenagers."

"They're her cousins," Cortez said tightly.

"Be that as it may, look at what happened." She waved a hand in the general direction of the upstairs. "Is this what happens when she comes to visit? You don't keep an eye on her?"

"I cannot watch her every second of every day, Nadine."

This time the beautiful pronunciation of her name lay buried under the weight of irritation in his voice.

"I knew you would overreact," he muttered.

She hated that word—*overreact*. As if there was something wrong with her for loving and caring deeply for her only child and wanting to ensure her safety at all times. After they'd lost their baby, he accused her of stifling their daughter. However, she saw it as simply being attentive.

"I am her mother. I am not overreacting."

"And I am her father."

"Then act like it," she snapped.

He flattened his palms against the gray granite countertop. "What would you like me to do? Follow her around everywhere she goes to make sure she doesn't skin a knee or bump a toe?" His accent thickened in frustration.

Nadine crossed her arms. "You know good and damn well that's not what I'm saying. You also know she shouldn't have been in the car with those other kids. An adult should have been driving them. Or she should have been in the car with you and your aunt and her husband."

"The car was full with my aunt and her family. Antonella wanted to ride with her cousins, and she was perfectly safe with her older cousin driving."

"Yet they had an accident."

"You do understand the other car—the one with the *adult* driver—ran through the traffic light and hit *them* in the side? Was that made clear to you?"

Nadine fisted her hand. "Don't condescend to me."

"And don't question whether or not I do what's best for Antonella."

"My daughter—"

"*Our daughter,*" Cortez growled, face tightening. His words hung in the room like bitter, rotten fruit. "Our daughter."

Nadine felt a twinge of guilt. "It was a slip of the tongue."

"No, it wasn't." A muscle in his jaw twitched. "You've always only thought of her as yours."

"That is *not* true."

"You came in here wanting to argue," he accused, jabbing a finger at her. His handsome features hardened, lines of tension deepening in a face already creased with fatigue. "You're not going to like what I have to say. Antonella is back in her home country, on familiar ground, where she belongs. When you left, you took the most precious thing I have in the world away from me and I accepted it. But do not push me, Nadine. Do not make me take her back."

Nadine's head jerked back and her stomach dropped at the blatant threat.

Leaving hadn't been easy. She recalled the heartrending sobbing as nine-year-old Antonella clung to her father one last time, refusing to get on the flight. Only after he insisted that she release him and go did she finally allow Nadine to take her through the gate to the plane. But Nadine had never forgotten the look on his face. The unshed tears in his own eyes.

She'd hurt him deeply the day she left with their daughter. The one thing she hadn't suspected was that Cortez had never forgiven her for it.

CHAPTER 11

"You don't mean that," Nadine said, one hand closing into a fist. "You won't keep her here."

"Don't be too sure." He'd been thinking about it for some time, and this incident had only brought the decision to a head. "I am tired of having to make appointments for video chats and weekly phone calls."

The emptiness ate at him, day in and day out. Phone calls were not enough. Seeing her once or twice a year was not enough. Not when she was growing and experiencing life—and all he had was the photos representing all the precious moments he'd missed.

"She's happy in Atlanta. She has friends and family and school there."

"She has friends and family here, too. For the first nine years of her life, this was her home, she went to school, and was perfectly fine. If you move back to Buenos Aires, we can both see her and spend time with her."

"I can't do that. I have a job."

"Then let Antonella stay."

Her eyes widened in panic. "That's not our arrangement."

"We never had an arrangement. You left and took her with you. I never had a say."

"Well, why would you now?" Nadine shot back. "You expect me to just—just leave her here? How can you suggest something like that, especially after I almost lost her?" Disbelief filled her voice.

"I almost lost her, too," Cortez reminded her in a low voice.

Her face filled with acknowledgement, and perhaps a bit of shame that she had completely ignored the fact that he, too, was still shell-shocked by the possible loss of their only child.

Her gaze dropped to her intertwined hands.

"I saw her get hit. I *saw* the car smash into the car she was in."

Cortez sank onto one of the chairs around the island and buried his head in his hands, reliving the real-life nightmare of the accident as it had unfolded in front of him. They were all fine, but he'd been seized by such unimaginable terror, he'd hopped out of the car he was driving while it was still rolling and rushed to get to the mangled sedan carrying Antonella. His uncle, who had been seated beside him, had been the one to apply the brakes to the vehicle to avoid another accident.

A soft hand squeezed his shoulder. She'd moved quietly, or perhaps he'd been so distracted he hadn't heard her come across to him.

"She's okay," Nadine said quietly. Her fingers kneaded his tight shoulder, offering much needed comfort.

Snaking a hand around her waist, he pulled her close,

and they bent around each other, burying their faces into each other's necks.

She rubbed her cheek against his stubbled jaw. Perhaps an innocent act, but one that woke up the sleeping longing within him. With a simple twist of his head, the side of his mouth tasted the corner of hers. She released a little whimper, an encouraging sound that made him press his lips more boldly against hers.

This kiss wasn't like the last one. During the last one, he'd been consumed with hunger and passion, driven by a burning need to possess her. This time he sought solace from the one person who understood how he felt.

Her soft mouth opened and his tongue traced the inside of her upper lip. She moaned and leaned into him, her fingers tightening in the hairs at the back of his head.

He squeezed her closer, pulling her between his legs and locking her in place. Pressed together, chest to chest, the thud of her heart beat against his, and he ached to lose himself inside of her and forget the past. Forget everything.

Cortez grasped Nadine's arms and lifted his head. Her startled gaze met his, and she licked her mouth—as if savoring the taste of him—forcing a quiet groan from deep in his chest.

"We're both tired. We don't want to make a mistake." He didn't release her. He couldn't just yet.

She nodded, struggling to get her breathing back under control. "A mistake. Yes."

"The stress. The lack of sleep."

She stepped back and his hands fell away from her arms. Her eyes skirted him and focused on other objects in the kitchen—the island, the glass of water that he'd been drinking.

"Lots of stress. We're both exhausted. We should go to bed. Not together," she added hastily. "I mean...separately."

"Of course."

Her eyes dipped to his crotch, and he made no move to hide his arousal. Her breath hitched and her eyes darted away again, finding other things to focus on in the room —the refrigerator, the bowl of fruit on the counter.

"Good night."

He watched her as she walked toward the door. "Nadine."

She paused and turned.

"Think about what I said."

Her face remained inscrutable and she didn't say a word. Then she turned on her heel and left.

CHAPTER 12

The SUV with Gustavo, his wife, and the other children pulled out the next morning after breakfast for the three hour drive back to the *estancia*.

Both Antonella and Gabriela suffered some muscle soreness from the accident, but for the most part they exhibited lots of energy, like typical girls their age. Nadine was impressed that the splint didn't inhibit Antonella's movements much at all.

Since the girls were fine, Cortez took them into town for lunch and a visit to the zoo. Nadine had plans as well. Joachim took her into the city where she met a friend for lunch that she'd kept in close contact with after she moved to Atlanta.

Catarina was in her early sixties, with fine lines on her face and hair died a glossy jet black, never marred by gray roots. Slender and chic, the older woman had become a close friend and confidante when they both taught at a local school—the job Nadine had found after she resigned from her position as an import/export consultant years ago.

Now retired, Catarina spent her days volunteering with various children's charities. She'd once told Nadine that it was her way to give and receive the love that bonded children to adults since she'd never married and had children of her own.

After a leisurely lunch at an Italian restaurant, they strolled down Florida Street. The busy area was close to the financial district, and only open to pedestrian traffic. Nadine wanted to buy leather goods and gifts for family back home.

"So when are you coming to visit me in Atlanta?" Nadine teased, as they walked arm-in-arm. She'd been trying to get Catarina to come visit for the past couple of years.

"Why would I leave all of this?" her friend asked, waving her hand with a flourish at the street, teeming with pedestrians carrying bags and browsing for gifts. "And why are you buying souvenirs here? You know better. This place is for tourists!"

Nadine squeezed her friend's arm. "I know I can get better deals elsewhere, but I like the energy here."

Catarina cast a sidelong glance at her. "Are you ready to come home?"

"Atlanta is my home now, and you're welcome to visit anytime. I'm sure you'll love it."

"You know I have no interest in going to the States." Catarina sniffed.

"Not even for a short trip?"

She shrugged, a movement that looked decidedly

elegant on her narrow shoulders. "Maybe a week. Maybe Alec would like to join me."

She and Alec, Cortez's longtime friend who'd gone to work for him at the record label, Musica Fuerte, had been lovers for almost ten years. They'd met through Nadine and Cortez, and their relationship had endured, despite the significant age difference.

"So you won't come unless Alec comes?" Nadine paused to examine a *yerba mate* tea set that included a bag of the loose tea leaves, traditional hand-carved gourds, and a pot for hot water. The set would make a nice gift for her neighbor. She made a mental note to come back to this store.

"I like traveling with him. He takes care of everything." Catarina laughed, the sound husky and mischievous.

"When are you going to marry him?"

"Maybe when he stops asking me."

"Then it'll be too late," Nadine scoffed. "Are you saying you don't want to get married?"

Catarina glanced sideways at her. "You were married before. What do you think? Would you do it again?"

They started walking.

"I enjoyed being married," Nadine said.

"Why aren't you anymore?"

"You know why. We couldn't make it work."

They strolled along in silence for a while, pausing long enough to toss change into the bowl of a couple of street performers dancing the tango.

"Alec says he no longer writes," Catarina said.

"Who?"

"Cortez."

Nadine stepped out of the way of a group of young

tourists that rushed past. "No way. Cortez never stops writing music."

When they were married, he must have written hundreds of songs. Some had been good enough to make the cut and onto his albums. Some had been filed away for one reason or another. Perhaps because he had another song that sounded too similar or another singer had released a similar sound and composition. Or, like all temperamental artists, he simply thought it wasn't good enough.

"Alec says he hasn't written anything in years."

Years? Even when they'd discussed him starting the record company, he'd insisted he'd continue writing.

"He's not alive if he's not writing." Of that she was certain.

"There is your answer," Catarina said.

Nadine pulled up short.

"What are you saying?"

"Maybe he's not alive." Catarina raised an eyebrow. "When does he see Antonella?"

"He sees her."

"Once a year."

Nadine disengaged her arm. "Did Cortez put you up to this?"

Catarina's eyes widened. *"No."* Her friend seemed genuinely shocked by the accusation.

"He's not the first parent to live apart from their child."

"I am not accusing you of anything, but I see how he is when she comes to visit on her summer break. He is so different when they are together. I thought...perhaps a compromise could be reached."

"He did put you up to this." She found it hard to

believe that it was only a coincidence that Catarina would broach the same topic that she and Cortez had discussed so recently.

"No, he did not," Catarina insisted.

"To guilt me into leaving her."

Catarina's brow furrowed. "Not to leave her. But... have you considered coming back?"

"Why should I move back?" Nadine demanded. "Maybe Cortez should move to the States."

"I am sorry. I have said too much, and I did not mean to upset you. I only know that Alec and I see how he is." She took Nadine's hand. "And of course I was sad to see you go and thought maybe you would return once you had the break you needed. I would love to have you come back, but I understand why you left and why you may never live here again." She looped her arm through Nadine's. "Come. No more of this talk. Only happy conversations for the rest of the day. Tell me about Atlanta. What is so great that Alec and I need to visit?"

Nadine let her friend pull her along. "Southern hospitality, to start."

She went into a half-hearted description of the weather and the historic neighborhoods, but her heart was not really in the conversation any longer. Her thoughts were all about Cortez.

CHAPTER 13

*A*fter the outing, Nadine returned to the house but didn't immediately find any trace of Cortez or the girls and went upstairs to place the gifts in her room. Then she went to Antonella's room and gently knocked. When there was no answer, she peeked in and saw the girls were already fast asleep in their individual beds. They were as inseparable as sisters.

With a satisfied smile, she went back to her room and changed out of her clothes. She took a quick shower before donning a comfortable loungewear outfit consisting of rose-colored pants with a drawstring and matching top. Sleep was the last thing on her mind. The conversation with Catarina, combined with Cortez's suggestion—or threat, depending on how she chose to interpret his words—had given her much to think about.

In the kitchen, she took a cola from the refrigerator and was on her way up the stairs when she decided to change direction. Pausing, she listened to be sure she didn't hear any activity nearby, and then walked quietly toward the back of the house.

She was curious about Catarina's comments that Cortez hadn't been writing music. The best way to find out the truth of that statement was to go to the home studio, his favorite room in the house—or at least it used to be.

Standing outside the door, she looked both ways down the hall before turning the knob.

Open.

She let herself in, but after such a long time, she felt like she was invading sacred, off limit turf, even though she'd been in there many times before. She eased the door shut and touched the control box near the door, illuminating the walls with soft overhead lighting.

The studio consisted of two rooms—the control room and the isolation booth—both with dark paneled, soundproof walls. Not a single window existed in the space, allowing Cortez to be completely sealed off from distractions. Against the right wall of the control room, four electric guitars were lined up on stands. To the left was a keyboard and, directly in front of her, earphones, a computer, and the equipment he and his producer used to monitor and mix beats.

She used to sit on the tan sofa against the back wall and read quietly while he worked on his music. Or sometimes she simply watched him, admiring his dedication and tenacity. When he didn't need to concentrate too much, she'd bring Antonella in the room with her, and he let her sit on his lap while he fiddled with the knobs and buttons. He had taught her to play the keyboard, and she'd continued piano lessons in the

States. The teacher had been impressed by her innate ability to play by ear.

Testaments to Cortez's talent over the ten years he'd been at the height of his singing career covered the wall above the sofa like wallpaper. They included Best Record, Best Album, and the various milestones in record sales—gold, platinum, and diamond. His ballads had won him the most accolades.

Nadine walked over to the keyboard and set down her cola. She ran her fingers lightly over the keys, reminiscing about those days. Every now and again she'd be flattered when he'd ask her opinion about a lyric or a beat, but for the most part he stayed busy and worked hard. For her, simply being allowed to spend time with him in the room where he created had been sufficient.

When she heard a click behind her, she spun around to see Cortez standing in the door holding coffee in his hand, steam rising from the white cup. Guilt flared in her stomach, as if she'd been caught trespassing.

Surprised to see her, Cortez initially had a bewildered expression on his face, but then his eyes narrowed with suspicion. "What are you doing in here?"

"I...was just curious." She sounded as guilty as she felt, poking around in his sanctuary.

One eyebrow arched higher. "About what?"

She might as well come clean. "I was in town with Catarina today, and I was surprised when she told me that you were no longer writing."

Without making much sound, he moved away from the door and it eased shut. He walked over to the table that contained the monitoring equipment and set down his cup of coffee.

"I suppose she heard that from Alec," he surmised.

Nadine was very cognizant of every gesture he made, each turn of his head, the sound of his deep voice. As if every action had been magnified for the benefit of her senses.

"That's what she said." Nadine leaned against the keyboard and looked around the room. "Did you stop writing because you got behind a desk?"

"No." He picked up a notepad on the table and stared down at the words written on the page.

She could have been put off by the shortness of his answer but refused to be. She had to know why he'd stopped doing something she knew he loved so much. "Then why?"

"I had my reasons."

"So you're never going to write again?" she prodded.

"I never said that." Tension sang in the taut set of his shoulders. "I'm writing now."

"Music?"

"Yes."

"So Catarina was wrong."

"Not quite. It's true I haven't written in a long time."

"But you're writing again? That's wonderful, isn't it? When did that start?"

He didn't answer right away, and she had the distinct impression that he was debating whether or not to answer her at all. Finally, he looked at her. "Today."

"Oh." The way he looked at her—in that steady, measured way—sent heat rising in her neck. "When was the last time you wrote?"

"Three years ago."

The admission and the dull sound of his voice pained

her. When she'd taken away Antonella, he'd lost his desire to write.

With great effort, she tugged air into her lungs. "What prompted you to do so now?" she asked in a low voice.

Cortez flipped a few switches, and soft music spilled from the speakers. "What do you think of this?" he asked.

It was a melodious, haunting sound. "It reminds me of pain. Maybe even loss."

"Longing. It's called *"Cuanto te amo." How much I love you.* He held up the notepad. "These are the words. You inspired them."

"You mean Antonella."

"No, Nadine. You."

adine's breath stopped. Her heart raced as she twisted Cortez's statement around and over in her head, and still it didn't make sense. "If this is some trick to try to convince me to let Antonella stay—"

He dropped the pad on the table. "This isn't a trick."

"Last night you told me you want her back, and today you tell me that you're creating music again because of me. You have to admit, that sounds suspicious."

There had been a time when he'd told her she inspired him to write his best work, but that had been a long time ago. Long before they'd turned on each other with petty arguments and long silences that drove them farther and farther apart.

"I am telling you the truth."

"I don't want you to make music about me."

"My biggest hit—my greatest selling single was a song dedicated to you—*about* you."

Mi corazón canta. My heart sings. An ode to how being

near her made him feel. She made his heart sing. Maybe once, a long time ago, but not in the end.

"Whatever you're doing, this can't happen. You know—"

"Why?"

"Because."

"Because what? We're not done, Nadine. Didn't you feel it when we kissed—the first time? The second time?" He tapped the notepad. "I wrote two songs already. They were going around and around in my head all day. I wrote one while the girls were in the pool, and I wrote the second after they ate dinner."

"You wrote two songs. I'm happy for you, but our marriage ended three years ago. *We* ended."

"You left me."

"We left each other," she flung back.

He shook his head. "I was still here."

"Were you?"

The chiseled plane of his jaw flexed. "I never wanted you to leave."

She laughed shrilly. "That is a damn lie and you know it. If you didn't want me to leave, why was leaving even on the table?"

"I gave you the option of a divorce. I didn't know you planned to leave the country."

"Why would I stay here?"

"Why not? This was your home for years. Our daughter was born here."

"Well, you didn't exactly fight for us to stay, did you?" Nadine said.

Cortez took two deep breaths, his chest heaving up

and down. "If I tried to make you stay, you would have resented me, and you were already so unhappy."

"And apparently so were you," Nadine said, the bitterness of his betrayal resurfacing on her tongue. "The minute I turned my back, you…"

"¿*Qué*? What did I do?"

"You and Fabiana made your relationship public!" A violent quiver of pain grabbed hold of her gut and twisted.

The blonde had been his favorite sound engineer when he was a performer. He claimed she was among the best, but Nadine had wondered if there was something more between them. She'd seen the way Fabiana looked at her husband.

An angry glint filled his eyes. "I told you over and over again there was nothing going on between us. I liked her work. That is all."

"I saw the pictures of you," she hissed. "Not even a month after Antonella and I left the country, you were partying with her in Ibiza."

Cortez averted his eyes and ran a rough hand through his hair. "I needed to get away."

"With her?"

An angry frown creased his forehead. "She came, but so did Alec and the rest of Los Tigres."

"They weren't the ones wearing a tiny white bikini on the yacht, laughing and hanging onto you!" Her heart thundered against her chest so hard she wouldn't be surprised if he heard it.

News about him hadn't been easy to come by in the States. As far as Americans were concerned, he was a one-hit wonder with the English translation of *Mi corazón canta,* but in Latin America and Europe he'd been a superstar. So she'd searched for news about him online, and that's when she'd found the pictures of him partying in Ibiza.

"Those photos were misleading," Cortez said between clenched teeth.

"Those photos were revealing," Nadine countered.

"You know how the press slants news stories to sell copies. How many times have magazine articles placed me in a particular restaurant or city on a specific date, when in fact you and I were together at the time? None of the rumors about other women were true. You know they weren't true."

"I *hoped* they weren't," she corrected.

His nostrils flared. "You're making excuses because you were unhappy. I never once strayed in our marriage!"

Nadine acknowledged to herself that she had conjured all sorts of explanations once their marriage started to crumble. If she was hardly having sex with him, was he getting it somewhere else? It would have been so easy for him because of his celebrity status.

"I was hurting, after…" She touched her stomach as the pain attacked her anew. The period after the death of their son had been the longest of her life.

His gaze dropped to her stomach, and his shoulders seemed to lower a full inch, as if a heavy load had suddenly been dumped on them. "You think I did not hurt, too?"

"When?" she whispered in disbelief. "When were you hurting? When did you ever show any emotion? You closed off from me and buried yourself in work. I never had any inkling about what you were feeling." Their conversations had devolved into monosyllabic inter-actions.

"Is that why you pulled away from me?"

"I never pulled away. You did. You hardly even touched me anymore." But when he did, she went up in flames.

Cortez pushed away from the table and stepped closer, too close for comfort. "I still wanted you, but there were times when I thought you were simply doing your duty as my wife."

Her eyes widened. "Did you think I was faking my orgasms?"

"I have no idea. I didn't know what to think."

"If you felt that way, why didn't you say something? Why didn't you talk to me? You hid behind your work and your traveling and you left me all alone."

"What should I have done?" he demanded. "Walked away from my music? It was the only way I knew to cope. It was important to me and there was a time when it was important to you, too. You were there, all along, supporting me. When I didn't make any money, you supported us teaching English. We built all of this togeth-er." He waved a hand to encompass the room.

She hefted a heavy breath past her lips. "I wanted to talk to you about...what was happening. But you worked harder. You did more shows, more studio sessions, more concerts. You never showed me you were hurt. You never showed me I could talk to you."

"I asked you all the time how you were doing."

"Over the phone—from a distance. From Bolivia. From Venezuela. From France. Sometimes I could hear fans partying in the background or women giggling and screaming. I wanted to see you. I wanted you to…hold me. Tell me it was going to be…okay." Her voice cracked. "You never said a word. You never showed me that you cared."

Cortez came closer. "So you thought the worst of me? That you married a cold, insensitive monster who didn't care about anyone or anything but himself? Not even the death of his own child?"

She winced at such an ugly characterization, staring down at the floor. "No. I just wish you'd shown more emotion. I felt like I was grieving alone." Pain throbbed in her voice.

The silence echoed around them, grating like an out of tune melody.

Nadine finally looked up at him, and her heart constricted at the raw emotion she saw etched in his features.

"The reason you never saw me grieve is not because I didn't care," he said quietly. "The reason you never saw me grieve is because…I was trying to be strong. For you."

$\mathcal{L}$ooking down into his ex-wife's upturned face, Cortez could tell his words surprised her. He rubbed his temple. "I didn't know how to help you, and you seemed to get all the care and consideration you needed from my family."

Immediately after she came home from the hospital, the women in his family had been attentive and considerate, forming a protective perimeter around her. They offered comfort, soothing voices, and a type of empathy and understanding that often made him feel he was in the way. Friends, family, band mates—everyone asked him how she was doing. After a few pats on the shoulder and murmured sympathetic words, no one inquired after his state of mind.

They may have been expecting, but *she* was the one who had lost a baby. Friends and family assumed she suffered from greater distress because of her physical connection to their child, so how could he compare his loss to hers? And what could he offer except trite platitudes?

So perhaps he had shut down. It was the only way he knew to cope with his grief and not inflict more heartache on her. He thought she'd needed strength, and as a result hadn't shown his own vulnerability. Now he realized what a mistake he'd made.

"For better or worse. Somewhere we went wrong," Nadine murmured.

They should have been able to make their marriage work, but their worse was more terrible than anything he could have imagined. The changes in her had torn him apart. She hadn't been the same woman he married—the one who laughed and teased or came to drag him out of the studio in the middle of the night because, as she put it, *Why am I sleeping alone even when you're in town?*

His mischievous, playful, sensual wife had been replaced by a depressed woman who'd jumped at the chance of divorce. Not once had she given any indication she didn't want that option. So when she dropped a bombshell and told him she planned to leave the country, he hadn't put up a fight. If being here made her so miserable, how could he in good conscience demand she stay?

"At the wedding, you asked me if I was happy. I wasn't completely honest with you," Nadine said.

He waited.

"I'm not happy, Cortez. I want to be, but I'm not." Tears shimmered in her eyes. "Not like I used to be."

"When we were together."

Her voice dropped even lower—so low he almost didn't hear her. "Before it happened."

Before the stillbirth.

The delivery had started fine, and they'd fully expected

to hold their newborn son in their arms. But the umbilical cord had compressed during labor, cutting off their son's oxygen and nutrients. She'd been forced to complete the delivery, knowing that he had already died. Still, Cortez had hoped that maybe the monitors and the doctor had made a mistake. Maybe when Cortez, Jr. came out, he would belt out a loud cry with strong lungs and prove everyone wrong. He'd seen the same hope in her eyes die the minute the doctor held up the tiny, lifeless body. They'd both been heartbroken.

"When we lost him..." Nadine's voice wobbled, and she pressed her lips together in an obvious attempt to keep them from trembling.

Cortez took her soft hand in his but remained quiet, giving her time to pull herself together.

Taking a deep breath, she continued. "Being in the public eye made the situation so much worse. I don't know how the press even got hold of the story."

"There are moles in the hospital—everywhere, really. Heartless people who can be bribed to divulge information for a few *pesos*."

News of the death of their son had been blasted in sensational headlines that worsened their private pain.

"I know." She nodded. "I—" He waited for her to gain control of her emotions. She opened her mouth again, but instead of words coming out, she burst into tears.

Cortez immediately pulled her into his arms.

"It's okay." He whispered soothingly to her in Spanish, rubbing her back as she quietly wept for a few minutes.

Sniffling, she lifted her head from his chest. "I'm sorry." She touched the damp spot on his shirt.

"It's not ruined." He swiped the dampness from her cheeks with the pads of his thumbs.

The gentle touch sent her body quivering into awareness, and Nadine stepped out of his arms. She needed distance, but when she looked up at him to make a run-of-the-mill suggestion about forgiveness, the intense way he looked down at her made the words stick in her throat.

"I couldn't sleep for months after you left me," he said softly. "This house...I hated it. I still hate it. Because you're not here. Do you have any idea what it's like for me to be apart from you and our daughter?"

"I have an idea." The past few years she'd hidden from the emptiness and longing, but coming back had made her face her feelings for him.

The air around them became charged, and her mouth suddenly became parched and desperate for moisture.

A spark of heat flashed in his eyes. "Nadine," Cortez groaned huskily. He sounded helpless. Overcome.

That was all it took. That husky, pleading sound of his voice touched a chord deep inside of her and dismantled any reservations she had.

They moved at the same time. Not one before the other, but simultaneously reaching for each other.

CHAPTER 16

*N*adine pressed against Cortez and wrapped her arms around his neck. Immediately, her body came awake with little firestorms of pleasure.

Their mouths fused together, his lips bruising hers in the intensity of the kiss. The rich, robust flavor of the coffee he'd drunk filled her mouth, along with the unmistakably unique flavor of Cortez.

Grabbing her bottom, he hauled her tight against his pelvis, and a silent gasp traveled up her chest, loins moistening at the erotic promise of his solid erection straining against her stomach. Her fingers burrowed into the lush thickness of his hair, holding him tight to get more. She wanted his mouth on her naked skin—licking and tasting with unreserved passion. Making her wet and hungry in the way only he knew how.

She sucked on his lip and grazed the sensitive inside with her teeth, eliciting a groan from deep inside of him. He shifted his head sideways and kissed her with all the sizzling desire that had been missing during the latter part of their marriage. They'd lost this ravenous, searing passion that consumed them both and had her pressed up against him so tightly they could have been bound together with industrial-strength glue. Cortez edged her toward the sofa and she followed his lead.

Later she wouldn't have any recollection of how they'd undressed. One minute she had clothes on, the next they were both naked and she straddled his powerful thighs on the sofa. The hard length of him extended between them and pressed against her belly like a long, hot rod, while his hands cupped and massaged her soft ass.

Their mouths reconnected, moving over each other in a deep, intimate kiss that stirred her blood and made the flesh between her legs pulse and ache. His hands glided up her sides and shaped the curve of her waist before skating even higher to cup her breasts. Her back arched as he squeezed them together and his thumbs glided in rough, deliberate circles around her taut brown nipples. He made them sting, he made them ache, and he had her so turned on she couldn't think straight.

His mouth joined the torture as he tongued the tips and nibbled on her sensitive flesh. Nadine arched her spine at an even deeper angle and he pulled her tighter against him, sucking one breast—devouring it, really—as though he wanted to pull the entire globe into his mouth.

"Harder," Nadine breathed, tilting her head back, losing herself in the suction of his mouth.

Cortez obliged. He moved to the other breast, sucking without mercy, and dragged his teeth along the hard peak the way that she liked. The act made her cry out and tremble from the unbearable ache of needing him.

He lifted his head and left a trail of moist heat on her

swollen breasts. His mouth climbed higher to her collarbone as one hand slid between her legs. His fingers massaged her lower lips, gliding in the moisture as he circled her swollen clit. A gasp tumbled from her lips and her body became even wetter under the caress of his fingers. Helplessly she twisted, moaning and gripping his hair. She should be worried about hurting him, but all she could do was hold on and draw him even closer.

Cortez licked behind her ear, the heavy rasp of his softly spoken words and the warmth of his breath wreaking havoc against the arch of her neck.

"I need you...Cort..." Nadine panted.

He whispered to her in Spanish, words of longing and praise, and the sound of his husky voice turned her impatient. She couldn't wait any longer. She was too desperate, too eager. With one hand on his shoulder and the other on his hard length, Nadine raised up on her knees and settled onto him in a slow, sensuous glide. He was thick and solid between her legs, and her wetness eased the entry until she was fully seated, forcing them both to let out husky groans that echoed in the quiet of the chamber-like room.

Fingers digging into his shoulders, she began to ride. She writhed on his hips, taking great pleasure in the power of his masculine form between her legs. Breathlessly panting, she felt almost reborn as she was bound to him so intimately again. Cortez gripped the soft flesh of her bottom and aided her movements up and down on his shaft. The noises in the back of his throat vibrated in the air and were the sounds of a man clearly indulging in the greatest of pleasures.

They continued to devour each other, compelled to do so by the basest of urges—luxuriating in a torment of moist kisses and sweet, demanding bites. Pushing the damp tendrils from his forehead, Nadine showered eager kisses on his face and tasted the familiar saltiness of his skin on her tongue.

The speed of their humping bodies increased to a more frantic pace, and the first sign of an orgasm stung in the base of her belly.

His eyes darkened with a lusty sexiness that made her heart trip and stumble in her chest. His lashes swept low as he concentrated, leaning back against the sofa to gain more leverage. With one hand on her waist and the other at the back of her neck, Cortez held her in place. His jaw set in a hard line. The muscles of his abs rippled as he worked his hips. He owned her, pushing air from her lungs with each mighty thrust.

The gradually unfurling tension abruptly released, and Nadine let out a small scream as ripples of pleasure burst throughout her entire body, sending shivers through every muscle. Breathing heavily, she fell forward against him and trembled as aftershocks rippled through her blood. Spent, exhausted, she felt annihilated from such a delicious, rigorous exercise.

Cortez stirred beneath her and that's when she realized he hadn't come. She lifted her head and searched his face. "You didn't…?"

"Not yet," he said in a grim tone. Before she could say another word, he maneuvered her onto her back.

The first time had been for her. How he managed to withhold his own climax, she had no idea, but by the determined set of his mouth, she knew that this time he aimed to get his own orgasm—hard and fast.

Cortez stretched her hands above her head and fastened his mouth over hers. The soft but firm movements of his kiss wrenched a moan from her chest, and Nadine parted her lips wider to accept his invasion. His tongue went deeper, tangling with hers, filling her with tingles as he stroked the roof of her mouth. He devoured her with a hunger that stole her breath and recreated tremors of pleasure down her hips and along her inner thighs. He had complete control of her now. She was beneath him and held down by him, and she whimpered in anticipation of what he would do next.

One hand continued to hold her prisoner as he hefted his heavy erection in his hand. Pressing her feet into the cushioned chair, Nadine angled her hips upward, seeking another orgasm and anxious to receive him.

He entered her without preamble. Swift. Hard. The action was punctuated by a low grunt and a Spanish curse. It was so sudden she didn't even have time to cry out. He drew back again and shoved into her. Her wet body welcomed him. Again and again. Using a slow tempo at first, and then increasing speed with rapid succession. All Nadine could do was fling her head back, mouth falling open as she took each pump of his body into hers.

The sofa creaked beneath them. The sounds of their harsh breaths filled the air.

She'd missed this out of control passion. She'd missed his hard body, missed the sensation of his hair-roughened thighs licking at the sensitive skin of her legs. She'd missed his mouth, his hands, his scent. She'd missed the way he made love to her. The way he made her feel— beautiful, desired, irresistible.

Heat flared in her abdomen and the pressure mounted inside of her again, each successive stroke compounded the pending climax. She tightened her legs around Cortez's lean waist, thrusting upward, thighs trembling as she strained toward satisfaction.

He gave her no reprieve, lowering his head to the beaded tip of one breast, tongue circling, teeth nipping, lips sucking on the chocolate nipple. The relentless torture of his mouth on her flesh was the final blow that sent her careening over the edge. With her body taut and arched in a silent plea against his mouth, she succumbed to the climax that assaulted the quivering flesh between her legs. Her voice cracked on a raw scream as wave after wave of ecstasy crashed over her body and flooded her senses.

Cortez followed behind, pumping so fast, his breath came in short spurts against the side of her neck. He grunted and his fingers bit into her wrists. Then a loud roar of satisfaction tore from his throat and his entire body shuddered before he collapsed on top of her.

Afterward, they lay facing each other, their breathing slowly returning to normal. Their sweat-slick bodies clung to each other, limbs intertwined to save space on the narrow sofa. One of Nadine's legs was trapped between his, and they each had an arm wrapped around the other. They were in that sleepy, satisfied state after great sex.

"Do you hear it?" Cortez asked, a husky, deep sound to

his voice. He brushed a thumb across her brow and flicked a damp tendril of hair behind her ear.

"Hear what?" Nadine asked.

He smiled at her. "My heart is singing," he whispered.

She melted. The onset of tears pushed against the corners of her eyes. "Me, too. *Mi corazón canta tambien.*"

CHAPTER 17

*I*f kisses were wine, Nadine would be drunk off the potency of Cortez's kisses right now. She was giggling, actually giggling, as he chased her onto the private balcony outside the master suite and trapped her against the ornate ironwork. Early morning quiet greeted them, the sun just beginning to break, casting orange rays to illuminate the scattered clouds in the sky. She'd always loved to watch the sunrise from this spot.

They'd been up most of the night and had not too long before taken a shower together. She wore Cortez's shirt, but he was completely naked, his hard body flush against her back, arms folded around her midsection in an embrace that was simultaneously sensual yet playful. She popped the last red grape from their platter of fruit into her mouth and laughed, tossing her head back as he growled in mock anger against the side of her neck.

"*Codiciosa,*" he said.

"I am *not* greedy. If I didn't eat it, you would have."

"What should I eat now, then?" he asked, his voice wickedly suggestive.

Nadine twisted her head around in time to see his lids lower to half-mast over his eyes. His hand slid between her thighs, and her breath hitched. Arching back against him, she rubbed her bottom against his crotch.

A low rumble erupted from his chest.

"I have something you can eat," she said.

"I bet you do."

Two fingers swirled in the moist cleft between her legs, and she released a long, heavy moan.

"This thing you have for me—is it moist?" Cortez asked, in a conversational tone.

Rocked by a shiver of pleasure, Nadine gripped the railing with both hands. "Yes," she choked out.

He inserted the two fingers into her body and she gasped and groaned louder, widening her legs and reaching back to loop an arm around his neck. His thumb joined in the mischief, flicking against her clit as his fingers continued to slide back and forth. Turning her face into his neck, Nadine trembled and whimpered his name.

"Have I ever had this thing you're offering?" The tenor of his voice dropped to a gruff, sexy drawl.

"Yes," she moaned, fisting her hand behind his neck. "You've had it plenty of times, and you love it."

He released her long enough to draw her into the room and strip his shirt from her body. Then they stretched out on the bed, and he used his mouth to take his fill between her legs. Her gasping cries countered his groans of pleasure, her trembling thighs held apart by his strong hands. His tongue tunneled into her, tasting the dew between her legs and delving into the wet crevices with enthusiastic groans.

She came apart with a quivering moan and had barely caught her breath when he rolled her onto her stomach. Her spine curled back to receive him, and he planted himself inside of her. The bunched-up silken sheets cushioned her breasts and teased her nipples with a delicate friction as over and over he pulled back and plunged deep, curling her toes and making her gasp out loud.

Each time he disappeared into her body, his hips smacked against the cushion of her ass. Cortez gripped her hips and squeezed, his fingers tightening in the tender flesh with each masterful thrust. And Nadine matched his long strokes, her uneven cries muffled in a pillow filled with his masculine fragrance, as he muttered under his breath in Spanish, voice guttural on each ragged draw of air.

Nadine's body broke apart for the fourth time in less than twenty-four hours, a powerful climax tightening her muscles and leaving her spent and gasping with Cortez collapsed on top of her.

His heavy body was a comfort she never thought she'd experience again. Tears came to her eyes as she considered how they'd drifted so far apart in their grief, but now she felt closer to him than she'd felt in a long, long time.

* * *

CORTEZ STOOD at the French doors watching Nadine sip a morning brew of *yerba mate* tea. She wore a pair of khaki-colored linen pants and a matching shirt. She'd slept later than usual today, but that had been his fault. For the second night in a row, he'd kept her up most of the night. He smiled to himself as he watched her. He wanted to shout from the rooftops, but they had decided not to let anyone else in the house know they were sleeping together. Partly because they didn't want to give Antonella false hope. She'd be happy if they reconciled, but this chapter in their relationship was too new.

They also savored the secrecy. They'd turned their little "affair" into a private game. She cast flirting glances at him over dinner. He pinched her bottom as he strolled through the kitchen on his way to the back yard.

Last night she'd slept in his room again. In the wee hours of the morning, she'd eased from the warmth of his body, and he'd slipped an arm across her waist, murmuring his discontent as he held her close for a little bit longer. Still, he didn't hold onto her for long. That was part of the game. So with a soft kiss he'd released her so she could get dressed. Before she sneaked from the room, she cast one last lazy, sexy glance in his direction, her face filled with undisguised affection. She left quietly, tiptoeing out the room to make the trek down the hall.

In two days she and Antonella would be leaving, and they needed to have a serious talk about their future. Even before that, they needed to discuss the one thing that he knew could send her spiraling back into her old ways.

"Are you going to stand there all morning?" Nadine asked without looking at him.

He walked over to the table and sat down. "How did you know I was standing there?"

"I always know when you're nearby," she said.

"How?"

"I feel it," she said simply. She smiled at him, her face glowing the way it used to. The happiness was slowly coming back, and he was almost afraid to broach the topic he wanted to. He didn't want to see those onyx eyes dulled.

She frowned and touched his face with a soft hand. "What's the matter? You look like you have the weight of the world on your shoulders."

"We need to talk."

Her hand fell away. "This must be serious." Already the light dimmed in her eyes.

"Before you get upset, I want you to hear me out." His stomach knotted. Talking about the death of their son was still difficult for him, and after she'd dodged the conversation last night, he knew it had to be done. "I want you to come see him."

Her face shut down, and she immediately scraped back her chair and stood.

Cortez stood as well, and caught her arm.

"I said no!" Nadine hissed. She yanked away. "Why are you bringing this up again? Why are you trying to hurt me?"

"I'm not trying to hurt you." He kept his voice level in the face of her stormy response.

She was shaking. "You asked me last night and I said no."

"It's been a long time since he passed, Nadine. You need to—"

"Don't tell me what I need to do!" she shouted. Her eyes had gone wild and her breathing erratic. She jabbed a finger at him. "You were not the one who had to—to…" Her voice shook.

"No, I didn't, but I was there." He remained steady and calm in the face of her agitation. "It killed me, too."

She pressed her hands over her face.

"Antonella has been to the grave with me," Cortez said quietly.

"What?" She stared at him aghast. "You took her there? Why?"

"Because she needed to know about her brother."

"She's a baby."

"She is not a baby. She's twelve years old and growing into a beautiful young woman who is smart and funny, just like her mother. Her first trip back, one of her cousins mentioned *júnior*, and she asked me about him. I explained what happened and I took her to see him. Every time she comes to visit, we go to place flowers on the grave."

"She never said a word to me."

"She didn't want to upset you."

Wringing her hands together, she digested that information.

Her dark eyes met his. "I don't think I can do it," she said in a low voice.

"You can." He took her hands and squeezed them between his. "You don't have to do this alone. I'll be there with you."

CHAPTER 18

*T*his was a terrible idea, and the closer they drove to the gravesite, the more apprehensive Nadine became. She absentmindedly tugged at the buttons on her shirt, not even aware she was doing it until Cortez took her hand in his to stop the fidgeting.

From the driver's seat, his eyes were filled with worry, but he smiled reassuringly. She couldn't manage to do the same and glanced out the side window, tightening her fingers around his hand.

She'd only been to the gravesite once, and that was the day of the funeral—the darkest day of her life when they placed their son in the ground. She hadn't cried that day. Not even once, remaining stoic in the face of whispered condolences from friends and looks of pity from family. Moving away to the States had dulled the pain to a much more manageable ache. But she idly considered that opening the door and flinging her body from the car would be far less painful than the enormous gaping hole of a wound that now threatened to engulf her.

When they pulled up outside the cemetery, she stayed in the car, still unsure if she'd made the right decision. Cortez walk around the front of the vehicle, opened her door, and extended his hand.

"Come," he said.

Pulling in a thick breath, Nadine exited the car and took his hand in a tight grip. Holding close to his side, she trudged along on lead feet. A gentle breeze rustled the leaves of the trees, and ahead of them on the path, an older woman knelt in the grass and placed flowers in front of a tombstone. Strange to think that a landscape so lush, with the grass spread out before them like a thick green carpet, housed death and sadness and gloom on every acre.

They walked for what seemed like miles before they arrived at the Alesini family plot and stopped in front of their son's gray marble headstone. Engraved in white letters was the date he died and written in Spanish, "In loving memory of our precious son Cortez Alesini."

Her body went numb to thwart collapsing under the pain, and her eyes misted over with unshed tears. "Do you come here often?"

"Not as much anymore."

Birds chirped nearby.

"It's not fair. He was so tiny." She drew in a tremulous breath. Could she have done something different?

As if he read her mind, Cortez said, "There was nothing you could do. Remember what the doctor said." He pressed a kiss to her temple.

Nadine lowered to her knees on the grass, kissed her palm, and pressed it to the top of the tombstone. Her head fell forward as grief overcame her. Cortez came down beside her and pulled her into his embrace, and for the second time in as many days, she cried in his arms.

This time she sobbed aloud, the wailing cry of a mother's loss. Tears streamed down her cheeks and dripped from her chin. Clinging to her ex-husband, she pulled the comfort and support she'd missed from him years ago. He held her close without a word until the sobbing stopped and no more tears fell.

The deep sadness she'd felt had been alleviated somewhat. The pain of losing her son still hurt, but Cortez had been right. She'd needed to come here to see the grave and properly grieve his passing. To finally move on.

They left soon afterward. In the car, his thumb rubbed back and forth across the back of her hand. She hardly noticed the scenery that whizzed by.

"You've done a good job keeping up his grave." Her voice was a little husky from crying, and she knew her eyes were red and swollen.

Cortez continued to rub his thumb across her hand.

"We need to keep it that way."

His thumb stopped moving and he glanced away from the traffic to look at her.

Yes, *we*. Did he understand what she meant? She finally felt ready to start again and would be coming back to Buenos Aires.

"I never stopped loving you," he said.

"Funny thing," she said with a watery smile, "I never stopped loving you, either."

She slid over and kissed his cheek.

* * *

CORTEZ GLARED at the door when a rap on the other side interrupted his phone conversation with the head of A&R. He'd given strict instructions not to be disturbed. The sooner he wrapped up this phone call, the sooner he could join Nadine and the girls at the pool.

"Hold on," he said into the receiver. He rose from the leather couch on one side of the office. Marching over to the door, he unlocked it and snatched it open. "*Sí.*"

On the other side, Philippa informed him that Fabiana Dietsch waited for him in the foyer and insisted on seeing him. Surprised by the unexpected visit, he didn't say anything at first. He hadn't heard from her since she took off for Germany months ago. Because of their history, and an odd expression on Philippa's face, Cortez was on alert.

"One moment." He went back to the phone. "I have everything I need for now. We can finish this conversation later." He hung up. "What's going on, Philippa?"

The woman's round face was creased in worry. "I think you should see for yourself, *señor.*"

With those ominous words, she took off, and Cortez followed her. On the way to the front of the house, he spotted Nadine and the girls at the pool. Antonella and Gabriela were splashing around, while Nadine sat in the shade on a lounger, reading a book.

He had to get Fabiana out of there. Her presence would only upset Nadine.

Fabiana, a slender woman of German and Argentine descent, stood in the open foyer wearing an orange pantsuit. Her ginger-colored hair was pulled back into a sleek updo that underscored her high cheekbones and narrow features. She looked almost exactly the same as the last time he'd seen her, except for one very major detail. She held a sleeping baby in her arms, bundled in a blue blanket and blue cap.

"Fabiana, what are you doing here?"

"*Mein liebling.*" Her gaze assessed him fondly.

The endearment took him aback. They hadn't seen each other in about a year, and she hadn't been so affectionate then. She'd been downright irate that he hadn't been willing to make a commitment. Hence the reason she'd quit Musica Fuerte and they'd gone their separate ways because, in her words, "she was no man's whore." He had understood her frustration but been unwilling to alleviate it because he hadn't wanted a relationship.

Fabiana was not the kind of woman he could see himself spending the rest of his life with, but she had been the ideal companion in two very specific ways. She looked great on his arm the few times they'd gone out, and she actually enjoyed attending the industry events. Because she'd worked in the music business for years, she knew a lot of the players and could comfortably hold a conversation with them on just about any hot topic.

"A friend told me your ex-wife is back in Buenos Aires." She made the statement calmly and without a flicker of emotion.

Cortez looked at the child and looked at Fabiana. "That's correct." Her presence made him uneasy, as if he shouldn't relax too much. "I didn't know you were back in the country."

"I have been back for some time. Keeping a low profile."

Very unusual for her. Fabiana liked to see and be seen.

"How was your trip? How are you?"

"Fine, considering."

She placed a hand on her stomach, the suggestive movement immediately sending a sensation like crawling ants down Cortez's spine. His eyes dropped to where her fingers lay splayed across her midsection.

"Considering...?"

"I came back to have a baby." A wide grin spread across her face, her features lighting up with excitement. In the depths of her eyes, he also saw hesitation.

"A baby?" Cortez croaked. He looked at her stomach, still covered by her hand, as if protecting the life that no longer resided there. His gaze landed on the child in her arms, and panic beat in his skull.

"Yes." She looked genuinely ecstatic. "As you know, I went to see my family in Germany, but I hadn't felt well the entire time I was there, and I went to see a doctor. That's when I found out that I was pregnant, and then our little tiff seemed so silly." She laughed easily, as if recounting the story to an old friend and not the man she'd shocked almost speechless with her news.

He couldn't believe how she'd mischaracterized their argument. She'd hurled insults at him—one of many being that he was still in love with his ex-wife, peppered with copious amounts of expletives. Even after they had calmed down enough to speak in reasonable tones, he'd seen the simmering anger in her eyes and the disappointment that he refused to offer her more.

"I want you to meet Erich Alesini," she said, coming closer. Still smiling, she walked over and placed the sleeping infant in Cortez's arms. He stared down at the child in bewilderment, examining the tiny nose, the plump cheeks, and the rosy little mouth.

His heart beat faster and something inside him shifted.

Traitorous feelings emerged from out of nowhere and filled his chest. Excitement. Joy.

"Isn't this wonderful?" Fabiana breathed. "Antonella has a little brother. And you have a son."

Cortez looked up, prepared to argue against what she'd just said, but caught movement from the corner of his eye. He turned and saw the last thing he'd ever wanted to see.

Nadine, with wounded eyes looking back at him from a stricken face.

CHAPTER 19

*F*abiana was gone, but her appearance had destroyed what little peace Nadine had managed to claim.

To think, hours after discussing a possible reconciliation and anticipating her daughter's squeals of excitement when she told her they'd be moving back to Buenos Aires, she discovered that her ex-husband had fathered a child with another woman.

"Congratulations." She barely got the words past numb lips.

"I don't know that he's mine." Cortez's voice was grave and emotionless. He stood beside the leather sofa in his office, watching her as she paced back and forth.

"You don't know that he's not." The bottom had officially fallen out of Nadine's little dream world. *Please let this be a bad dream.* Maybe if she pinched herself she'd wake up.

"Nadine—"

"This is what you wanted."

"*No.*" The fingers of both his hands tensed into tight fists.

"Maybe not with her, but you wanted another child." She knew the truth, even if he denied it.

"*We* wanted another child. You and me."

She let out an uneven breath, fighting the jealousy and hurt of knowing Fabiana would give him what she couldn't.

"This shouldn't change anything between us," Cortez said.

"Is that what you think?" Nadine laughed softly. Everything had changed as far as she was concerned.

"Just because she had a baby doesn't mean that you and I can't—"

"*She* didn't have a baby. You both did. Can you honestly tell me that some part of you isn't excited about being a father again?"

He ran a hand through his dark hair. "I don't know what I feel."

"You know exactly what you feel." She saw the guilt as it flooded his eyes. He didn't want to be happy, but some small part of him was. "You don't want to say the truth because you're worried about hurting me."

"We're going to work through this."

"How? I don't even know if I can trust you. You lied to me."

"I never lied to you."

"You said there was nothing going on between the two of you."

"When we were married," Cortez clarified. "And immediately after the divorce, the photos in Ibiza meant nothing."

"You conveniently omitted telling me you had an affair with her. Her, of all people!" She didn't expect him to live like a monk, but the thought of him and Fabiana together twisted her insides.

"It wasn't an affair. It was...nothing. A moment of weakness."

"Is that the euphemism men use now when they screw other women?"

His cheeks flushed dark red. "I regretted it afterward."

"Too bad you didn't stop before it happened."

Cortez took a step toward her, his body taut with tension. "I made a mistake. I am not proud of it. It shouldn't have happened."

"How many times did you make that mistake? How many times did you have a moment of weakness with her?"

"Nadine..."

"Tell me. I want to know." She tilted her chin higher, bracing for the answer.

"I can't recall."

"So did you regret it every time you did it?" she asked snidely.

His jaw hardened, but he didn't respond.

Pacing away from him, Nadine crossed her arms over her chest. She stared out the window at the plush grounds. There was a good view of the lake from here. The sun turned the surface of the water into sparkling jewels. The sight pained her, knowing she may never see it again.

Twisting around to face Cortez, she asked, "Why her?"

He sighed. "No specific reason," he said in a heavy tone. "Why not her? She was here. She was available. She was willing. And I was—" A vein in his temple popped into prominence. "Alone."

"So you'd have me believe."

"It's true. I had needs, Nadine."

"Obviously," she said bitterly.

Silence filled the room as they both eyed each other, and Nadine felt her happiness slipping further away, as her heart filled with pain and dread.

Finally, Cortez's voice broke through the quiet. "She and I went out a few times to industry events, but the night that we were…intimate…was the anniversary of our divorce. I was not in the best mood on that particular night. Thinking too much, drinking too much. I'm not making excuses, but…" He shrugged. "I hadn't been with anyone since you left me, and I haven't been with anyone since the night with her."

"Are you telling me that you haven't had sex with anyone else except Fabiana?"

"I am telling you the truth when I say that."

"What about the telenovela actress you were dating a few months ago? And the Brazilian socialite whose daughter wanted to be a singer? There were rumors about the two of you having an affair."

"You seem to know a lot about my personal life," he said quietly.

Nadine's cheeks burned with embarrassment. "I can't help it if occasionally I catch a story about you in the tabloids."

"The American tabloids? I barely make the press here anymore, so somehow I doubt that's true." He didn't have to say anything else. They both knew she'd been checking up on him. "I didn't have a relationship with any of those women. Whatever you heard or read is incorrect. Except for Fabiana, there has been no one."

She hadn't expected that answer. "In *three years*?"

"That is correct. I know you find that hard to believe, but it's the truth."

The thought that his periods of abstinence had anything to do with her was an enticing thought, but the issue of Fabiana still hung over their heads.

Nadine stared down at her fingers. "I can't watch you with your new baby, and Fabiana is going to need your support. You're going to be a father again. You should be celebrating because this is a happy occasion."

Cortez came toward her. "Don't make any final decisions yet. We were talking, we were making love." He cupped her face, his long fingers fanning over her cheeks, a burning urgency in his eyes. "We can figure this out together. We can work through it."

She pulled his hands away from her face. "No, we can't."

"Yes, we can. I love you." The desperate tone of his voice lashed her conscience.

She couldn't look at Cortez's joyous face when he held his son in his arms, and she knew she'd hurt him with the next words, but she couldn't face Fabiana. Seeing her would be a reminder of her own failures and her own loss, one that she'd only newly come to accept.

Nadine shook her head vehemently. "If Erich is your son, we can't work through this, because you're ignoring an important fact." He was asking too much, and there was no point in lying to him. "I won't want to."

His face shuttered at the finality of her words.

CHAPTER 20

*S*tuffing his hands into his pockets, Cortez stared out the window of Fabiana's luxury apartment. The two-bedroom, two-bath was situated on a quiet street in Recoleta, the most affluent neighborhood in the city. A few blocks over was the famed Recoleta Cemetery, a popular tourist attraction that contained the graves of prominent people—Eva Perón, presidents of Argentina, and even Napoleon's granddaughter.

The large, rectangular living room appeared more spacious because of the high ceilings—from which suspended an extravagant chandelier—and ivory walls, simply decorated with a large framed photo of Erich on one side and six small black and white framed photos of Argentina's main tourist attractions on the other.

At the tap of Fabiana's heels on the hardwood floor, Cortez turned around. She'd just put Erich down for a nap after his feeding.

"He's fast asleep," she said.

She appeared a little anxious, twisting her fingers

together even though she smiled as she approached him. No doubt she picked up on his serious mood, despite his playfulness with Erich earlier.

"We have to do this," he said.

"We don't have to do anything." Her face tightened into an unnatural smile.

"Enough," Cortez said through gritted teeth. He didn't want to argue with her. He didn't want to fight. He simply wanted answers.

"Forgive me if I want to pretend that my ex-lover isn't accusing me of being a whore."

"I never called you a whore." And did one night really constitute being lovers?

"Isn't that what it means when you question a woman on whether or not the child she carried is yours?" She placed both hands on her hips and stared at him. "Did you question Nadine and suggest that Antonella is not yours?"

"Of course not."

"Of course not. Oh! *Meine güte*, your perfect American wife would never betray you with another man. Are you so sure about that?" She tilted up her chin in defiance.

"Antonella is mine," he said evenly, refusing to let her bait him into an argument about the paternity of his daughter.

"Erich is yours."

"I need proof."

"You insult me." Her eyes flashed in anger.

"The longer you delay, the more I doubt."

"Because you want to go back to your ex-wife!" she spat. She marched over to the wall, arms crossed, and stared at the photo of her son.

"Are you sleeping with her?"

"That's none of your business."

Fabiana swung to face him, strain evident on her face. "You are, aren't you?"

"None of your business." Cortez struggled to keep his temper in check, but he would not allow her to stray off topic. "If Erich is my son, I want to know without having any doubts."

"Don't you love him?"

"I want to know without a doubt—"

"Do you love him!" she screamed, shaking, fists clenched. Her face crumbled, the wound of his rejection open and plain to see.

The boy was animated and lively, and his smile was like turning on a light in a dark room. But Cortez had to know the truth. He couldn't give of himself completely with doubt niggling the back of his mind, like a bothersome pebble in the bottom of a shoe.

Tears swelled in Fabiana's eyes. "He is yours." Her voice wobbled.

"If you don't come with me, I'm taking him to a doctor and having the test done myself."

If she came, too, they could also test her. Having the mother also do a swab made the tests more conclusive, but it was clear she wanted to put up a fight.

Fabiana stared down at the floor.

"He deserves to know who his father is," Cortez said. "His father deserves to know him. Is Erich my son?' His stomach tightened in the ensuing silence.

Watery eyes looked up at him. "I don't know."

Cortez stilled. "Why don't you know?" he asked in a perfectly controlled voice.

She licked her lips. "I was angry at you for rejecting

me, treating me like that night we spent together meant nothing." Her cheeks reddened in humiliation. "You just tossed me aside when you were done."

"I never tossed you aside."

"Yes, you did!" The fingers of one hand curled into a fist. "You used me to make yourself feel better because of *her*." Her voice was filled with bitterness and anger. "Then you just let me go. So I slept with someone else. While I was in Germany, I discovered I was pregnant."

"You've known all along he could be the father."

"Yes," she admitted, shamefaced.

Cortez wanted to smash something. Instead, he asked, "Where is he now?"

"He lives in Palermo."

"Who is he?"

"A friend of a friend. No one, really. He's nothing like you. He has no money, no..." Her voice trailed off as the avaricious reason behind her focus on Cortez revealed itself.

He turned away so she wouldn't see the utter disgust in his face.

"It's not just about the money, Cortez. You know that. I have feelings for you."

He twisted back in her direction. "And you hate Nadine, though she has never done anything to you." Fabiana had used Erich as a ploy to drive away Nadine and sink her claws into him. More than ever he regretted his weakness that night. His need to forget and seek comfort had caused him to make a grave mistake.

Fabiana curled her upper lip. "You act as if she is so perfect. She *left* you. I would have never done that."

Cortez took two steps toward her, anger coursing

through him with the speed and strength of a lightning bolt. Fabiana looked up at him with defiance, but she took a step back.

"Have nothing to say about my wife," he said in a dangerously quiet voice, enunciating each word so there was no misunderstanding. Nadine *was* his wife. Their divorce and time apart had not diminished his love for her, and he knew in his heart no one could ever take her place. "Especially when you had the audacity to show up at her house, unannounced, claiming me as the father of your child when you know there is another possibility. Nadine would *never* do that."

Fabiana's cheeks blushed a bright red.

Cortez rolled his neck to relieve the tension. "The sooner we get this straightened out, the better. I'll call you with the arrangements, and in a few days, we'll know the truth."

Fabiana lowered her eyes to the floor again. "All right," she said in a whisper.

After one last glance at her, Cortez left.

CHAPTER 21

*N*adine watched Cortez detailing his motorcycle in the driveway. He rubbed conditioner into the hand-stitched leather seat, his movements slow and careful. He could have one of his employees do it, but he loved that gold and titanium beast of a machine. He'd had it custom-made and imported from Ecosse not long before they split.

She had to admit, the motorcycle was a thing of beauty. Back when he'd bought it, she'd remarked that he must be going through an early midlife crisis, but he'd been undeterred by her comments and even invited her to ride with him. She'd refused, complaining that it was too dangerous. And what would Antonella do if something happened to both of them?

Fabiana's visit yesterday had created a mild rift between them—one she still didn't quite know how to overcome. This morning he disappeared without saying where he was going, but she couldn't help but wonder if he'd gone to see her and his...alleged son. The thought of losing the little closeness they'd managed to recapture needled her chest.

She walked onto the driveway and Cortez looked up from buffing extra cleaner from the seat. "I don't think you can shine it anymore," she said.

Holding the microfiber cloth, he stepped back and surveyed his handiwork. The sunlight glinted off the titanium, and the leather looked as new as the day he'd purchased the bike.

His mouth twisted at the corner. "You're probably right."

"Do you ride often?"

"Every now and again."

She came a little closer. "You're taking it out now?"

He nodded and warmth entered his eyes. "Come ride with me."

"No way." Nadine laughed a little.

"Why not?"

"You're not serious."

"Yes, I am."

She pointed. "That thing is not safe."

"Then why did you let me buy it?" As if she could have stopped him.

"You talked me into it. You can be very persuasive." Just like he'd convinced her to marry him and adopt this country as her home.

"Can I be very persuasive right now?" The wrinkles at the corners of his eyes deepened as he smiled. "The old Nadine would ride with me."

She placed her hands on her hips. "Are you challenging me?"

"I'm challenging the old Nadine to make an appearance. I know she's still in there—somewhere," he needled.

She had an overwhelming urge to be close to him, to recapture some of what they'd had before Fabiana's reappearance. "Promise not to go too fast."

"I promise. You'll be safe with me."

Fifteen minutes after he gave her a few pointers, Cortez handed over a gold and titanium-colored helmet to match the bike. He chose to ride without one, donning only a pair of dark sunglasses to protect his face. He looked sexy in an older, rock-star kind of way—with the shades, black T-shirt, and his muscular thighs clad in a pair of worn jeans, straddling the big steel horse. Nadine placed her hands on his hips, her heartbeat pounding erratically with a combination of nerves and excitement.

They pulled out of the driveway, onto the neighborhood street and rode through the development. Through the security gate they went and onto the roadway. She had no idea where they were going, but as promised, Cortez cruised along at a moderate pace through traffic. He maneuvered the vehicle with such finesse and ease Nadine's fear diminished and she relaxed and enjoyed the ride.

Riding a motorcycle was a completely new experience. Without the metal insulation of a car's protection, she had a heightened sense of awareness of the environment around them. Wind brushed across her arms and denim-covered legs, and she felt every dimple and turn in the road. She even smelled the freshly mowed grass they passed and the roasting meats and fragrant spices from the open doors of restaurants.

They traveled the very busy Avenue de Mayo in the

heart of the city, and followed it down to Plaza de Mayo. It was the city's main square and commemorated the beginning of the revolution in the country's independence from Spain. Argentina was known for their protests as much as the French, but surprisingly there were no protesters that day. Only tourists milled around, snapping photos and taking selfies with the obelisk in the center as a backdrop. Feeling particularly light-hearted, Nadine waved at them and some waved back.

They wound their way through cars and past the government buildings and towering hotels—modern structures dropped into the cityscape to accommodate the many visitors that arrived every year.

Then they went outside the city, away from the traffic and the noise. Out on the open road, Nadine felt freer than she'd felt in a long time. Like a shot of caffeine in the veins. She even let out a little whoop and tossed her head back.

She felt the tremble in Cortez's belly as he laughed, and when he turned his head to the side, she saw his face had softened into a smile. She couldn't help leaning into him, pressing her breasts against the strength of his back. She reveled in their closeness and the joy of the moment as the wind whipped around them. She blocked from her mind the possibility that anyone could take this away from her. This oneness with him, the machine, and the open road.

On the way back, the sun was going down, and Nadine held on tight, breasts taut and swollen now. Bowed across his back, a sense of peace and tranquility filled her spirit— something she hadn't experienced in Atlanta In all honesty, the only time she ever felt this way was in Argentina with Cortez.

She closed her eyes and for a moment she recalled the early days of their marriage—just the two of them against the world. Fighting together for his success. Celebrating with each unit of a song sold. Holding hands and smiling at each other when someone recognized him or shyly asked for an autograph. At the time, it had all been so new and exciting. Everything they'd sacrificed had finally paid off and he had become the successful singer he'd always dreamed of being. Even bigger and more popular than they'd ever imagined.

With the hum of the engine and wind gliding across her limbs, Nadine inhaled the leathery scent of the bike and the maleness of Cortez—selfishly wishing, just for a moment, that those days of struggle and excitement had never come to an end.

CHAPTER 22

*T*omorrow. They would leave him tomorrow.

Cortez brushed his hand over Antonella's thick curls. She sat wedged beside him in her pajamas on the sofa. They were in the living room where he, she, and Gabriela watched television. Gabriela sat on the chair perpendicular to the sofa with a morose expression on her face. She was going to miss her cousin.

"You have to go to bed so you can get up in the morning," Cortez said quietly.

Antonella shook her head stubbornly, refusing to budge from his side.

This happened every time she came for a visit. She never wanted to leave. He never wanted her to leave. They should be used to the ritual by now, but it only grew more painful each time.

"You'll be back in the winter," he said.

She always visited for a month in July during her summer vacation, the middle of winter here. Maybe by then Nadine would have forgiven him for what he'd done, and he could try again to convince her to come back. For them to start over. Even if Erich was his son.

His head fell back against the back of the sofa at the futility of his thoughts. He couldn't do that to her. He'd made his bed, and now he had to lie in it.

"Come on, you two. Let's go."

Cortez turned off the television.

"Papá." She didn't have to say another word. The despair came through loud and clear in her pleading tone. Antonella's eyes, beautiful and dark like her mother's, implored him to do something. To make this visit different.

He wanted to fight and yell at the unfairness of the situation, but he had to be an adult. Be firm with his daughter, knowing it would be another six months before he could touch and kiss her sweet face again.

He cradled her head in his palms. "The time will go quickly. Before you know it, you'll be back again, okay?"

She nodded, but her lower lip trembled as she tried to keep from crying.

He took both girls upstairs to Antonella's room and made sure they climbed into their beds. When he left them, they were under the covers, but he suspected they wouldn't go to sleep anytime soon. Last year he'd peeked into the room on the last night and found them wide awake, sitting on Antonella's bed, talking.

He hesitated at Nadine's bedroom. It was dark under the door. She was probably fast asleep. Antonella took after him in that she didn't need much sleep. Nadine, on the other hand, preferred to get as much as eight hours per night, and since they had to leave early in the morning, she was probably already asleep.

He proceeded down the long hallway and around the corner to his suite, his thoughts on the bike ride this afternoon. The pervasive loneliness he'd grown accustomed to had been temporarily alleviated—if only for a little while. He loved when his daughter came to visit, but having Nadine here, too, had made this particular trip that much more special.

In his room, Cortez changed into pajama pants and lay flat on his back on the bed. He stared up at the dark ceiling. Reflecting on the close moments they'd shared, the room seemed to fill with the sound of her laughter. He saw her smiling at him as she popped the last grape in her mouth. Then he saw her beneath him, begging him to prolong the pleasure. Begging him not to stop as he sank deeper and deeper.

Could he give it all up? Hadn't he done that before—given up, because he thought it was the right thing to do?

What had she said in the studio? *You didn't exactly fight for us to stay, did you?*

Cortez sat up, heart darting into a faster pace.

Essentially, he was repeating the same behavior by letting her go without a fight because he thought it was the right thing to do. But it wasn't. Not when they loved each other.

He hopped off the bed, intending to barrel down to her room and wake her up. But when he yanked open the door, Nadine stood on the other side, dressed in a loose-fitting pair of shorts and matching tank top, hand in the air as if she was about to knock.

Cortez didn't ask any questions. He already knew why she was standing outside his bedroom door. He saw it in her eyes.

He pulled her into the room and slammed the door.

Nadine backed into the wall. "It's going to be hard," she whispered, her voice pained and trembling. She swallowed.

Cortez walked slowly toward her, holding her gaze. When he stood directly in front of her, he held her face in his hands, rested his forehead against hers, and closed his eyes.

"Nadine," he breathed.

"But you're mine. You're *my* husband." Her voice sounded stronger. "If Erich is your son, we'll work through it. I—I don't want anything or anyone to come between us again."

Cortez lifted his head. "Are you sure you can work through this?" he asked, even though he'd been about to go to her room and ask her to do that very thing.

She nodded.

"Say it," he said in a hoarse whisper. "I need to hear it. Tell me when you leave here, you're coming back. Tell me you won't make me live another year without you. Tell me again that you love me."

She smiled through the tears. "I'm coming back. I can't live another year without you—the man that I love. *Mi esposo.*" She'd called him her husband.

Cortez's hand slipped into her soft hair. Dragging her tight against him, he kissed her.

The reason his love life had been so barren since the divorce—why he hadn't pursued a relationship with the telenovela actress, the Brazilian socialite, or any woman, for that matter—was because they weren't *this* woman.

Cortez groaned as he kissed her, tenderly at first, the velvety softness of her lips moving slowly under his. He groaned, pressing his mouth harder against hers, and she kissed him back with an equal amount of fervor.

No other woman looked like her. Not a single one of them made his heart race, his blood boil, or forged an automatic smile onto his face. Not a single woman in his entire life had ever made him want to write music, sing out loud, or slow dance in an empty room, just the two of them. No one but his Nadine, the woman who'd captured his heart and held it firmly in her possession since that day in the café.

He pushed down her shorts and hauled her underwear with it. As she pulled the top over her head, he fastened his mouth over one full breast and the nipple sprang to a hard bud in his mouth.

By the time she'd tossed the top aside, he had her against the wall, sucking her very delicious breast, her moans like music to his ears as her fingers tossed his hair into disarray.

They maneuvered down his zipper and lowered his pants, and he pressed her into the wall. With her bottom seated in his hands, he surged up into her wet flesh, her gasp right in his ear.

"*Mi esposa,*" he rasped. "*Hasta que la muerte nos separe.*" *Til death do us part.*

Their hips rocked together, chests pressed up against each other, her legs tight around his waist. Her fingers clutched his shoulders and her breathy whispers of incoherent words spurred him on. With each thrust, his body tightened and edged toward a total lack of control.

He felt the moment she came undone in his arms, even before her impassioned cry alerted him to her orgasm. She chanted his name as if they were the words to a song. The heart of her clutched him, the tight, wet heat too good to withstand.

With a brusque grunt, his body stiffened, and he join her in his own intense climax.

* * *

As they lay in the bed together. Cortez kept both arms wrapped around Nadine. He didn't want to let her go or wake up and learn this was a dream.

"When do you find out if he's yours?" she asked. Her breath brushed his collarbone.

"We take the test on Monday and we'll know in a few days."

She went quiet, and he threaded his fingers through her soft hair. He smoothed the short strands away from her face.

"Antonella and I will stay a few extra days."

"What about school and work?"

"She'll be fine, and I'll call my boss and let him know there's been a delay."

He brushed a thumb across her cheek. "I wish...I don't want you to be hurt by this. I will do my best to protect you."

"You don't have to protect me," she said quickly. She gazed at him with such love in her eyes, he had no doubt of her sincerity. "We'll face it together. We can handle anything together."

Shaking his head in disbelief, Cortez asked, "Have I told you how much I love you, *mi esposa?*"

He nuzzled her neck.

He heard the smile in her voice when she spoke. "You might have mentioned it."

EPILOGUE

Eleven months later

From the kitchen, Nadine looked out at the dramatic sunset on the back patio and pressed her face into the baby's neck, inhaling his scent of baby and powder.

"He is getting so big," Philippa said, a wide smile on her face.

"Pretty soon I won't be able to carry him." They both laughed. "You're almost ready?" Alec and Catarina were coming by later for dinner. Tomorrow, they were all heading out to Gustavo's *estancia* for the weekend. Cortez's parents were celebrating their fiftieth anniversary.

Philippa nodded. "*Sí, señora*. Go sit down. Rest. And don't worry about anything." She shooed Nadine from the kitchen.

With a soft chuckle, Nadine hurried from the room. She bundled her son in a white blanket and put a soft hat on his head before stepping out into the crisp spring air. He liked to be outside and gurgled happily against her breast, gnawing on his fisted fingers as he examined the environment.

Nicolás Alesini had arrived six weeks early on a cool winter's night in August. At three months old, he was a bundle of energy, kicking fearlessly and smiling with a beautiful, toothless grin.

Although she suffered from sleep deprivation, she couldn't be happier. If she never slept again, she'd be just fine.

"Where's my little man?" Cortez's voice boomed behind her.

"I don't even think you see me anymore," Nadine teased.

"Of course I do," he said, lifting Nicolás from her arms. He planted a soft kiss on her lips and then held out a wrapped box she hadn't noticed when he first appeared. "A little something for you."

"What's this about?" She held the box to an ear and shook it.

"*Nada mucho.*" He shrugged.

"Your idea of nothing much is not the normal person's idea of nothing much." The other day he'd bought her a new Audi in glacier white, because he wanted her to have something safe to drive the kids around in if Joachim wasn't available. That had been a *nada mucho* gift, as well.

She opened the box and inside was a bracelet with three gold discs, each embedded with a birthstone of one of children—a ruby for Nicolás, a pearl for Antonella, and an emerald for Cortez, Jr.

"It's gorgeous," she whispered. "Thank you."

After fastening the bracelet around her wrist, she pulled his neck down and gave him a loud, appreciative smack on the lips.

They sat on one of the cushioned benches, and Cortez rocked his gurgling son in his arms.

The past year had been busy, to say the least. The first hurdle they'd crossed was getting the test results to determine if Erich was Cortez's son. A courier had hand-delivered the envelope, and she and Cortez had sat together on the sofa in his office, holding hands. When he'd opened the envelope, her eyes focused right away on the words *is excluded as the biological father*. She'd never known such relief.

Fabiana had tried to claim Cortez as her son's father when she found out the real father couldn't financially support her the way she wanted. She'd hoped to cause a rift between Nadine and Cortez by offering Cortez a child. Her plan failed. Miserably.

Furthermore, two months after her return to Atlanta, Nadine discovered that the persistent queasiness she'd experienced for two days straight were symptoms of an unforeseen pregnancy. She and Cortez had not exactly been careful each time they made love, but being that they'd had difficulty conceiving before, this baby had come as a surprise.

Her excitement was second only to Cortez's. By the time he'd arrived in Atlanta to move them back to Argentina, the entire Alesini family was preparing for the baby. She'd stayed busy, nervous even though she knew that the chances of having another stillborn were statistically very low. She worked with an assistant—whom Cortez had insisted on hiring and which she eventually was glad he did—getting Antonella back in school, going on doctor visits, preparing the nursery, and planning a wedding. Cortez had been adamant that they be married before their son was born, and Nicolás had almost spoiled their plans, arriving only two days after their small wedding.

Antonella came racing up from the shores of the lake, where she'd been feeding the ducks.

"Hi, Nico." She kissed her little brother on the cheek. She looked forward to the days when he would be walking and talking and promised to teach him how to horseback ride and roast marshmallows on an open fire.

Nadine scooted over and her daughter plopped down between them.

She looked over Antonella's head at Cortez, holding their son who'd settled against his father's chest and fallen asleep. Cortez reached over and brushed her cheek with his free hand. She kissed his fingers and then looked out again at the sunset.

The vibrant reds and oranges that dyed the evening sky had recaptured her attention. She smiled to herself. Content.

She was home.

Excerpt from
Passion Rekindled (Brooks Family #2)

Sylvie Johnson stared at the sketches that one of her in-house designers had brought in. Holding them at arm's length, she examined the drawings of bold oranges and blues planned for next year's spring line. None satisfied her.

"No." She shook her head. "No, no, no." Sighing heavily, she tossed the sketchpads onto the neat desk, a uniquely modern creation she designed herself, made of a slab of glass on top of white concrete legs.

Sylvie glared at Roselle over black designer glasses. "These are horrid. I don't want to see you in my office again until you have something so exquisite I don't regret hiring you." She dismissed the young woman with a tight smile.

"Yes, Miss Johnson."

Roselle grabbed the pads and bowed her head in deference. The act grated on Sylvie's nerves, and she fought the urge to cringe. On more than one occasion she'd told Roselle to stop with the reverential bowing. She wasn't a queen, for heaven's sake, but she also knew that she intimidated the young woman.

Roselle lacked backbone but was sweet. Too sweet. The kind who'd get gobbled up by the vultures of the world if she wasn't careful. She created beautiful designs when pushed, but unfortunately did not dress the part.

Sylvie assessed the young woman with a critical eye. A purple shift dress hung off her bony shoulders, and her narrow face was—with a gray pallor beneath the cinnamon-brown skin—surprisingly gaunt. Roselle looked as if she was not taking care of herself and hadn't eaten in months.

"Roselle," Sylvie called out as the young woman rushed toward the door.

She turned, eyes wide, clutching the sketchpads to her chest.

"Have you eaten today?"

"I...um..."

"I will take that as a no." Sylvie removed her glasses and placed a fist on her hip. "We've talked about this, remember? You must nourish your body or your mind will suffer the consequences. Since I need your mind in tiptop shape—after all, that's what I'm paying for—I need you to take better care of yourself."

"Yes, ma'am," Roselle mumbled.

Sylvie shuffled papers on her desk. "Have Inez order you a meal from the restaurant across the street. Tell her to place it on my bill and order the usual for me, as well."

"Thank you."

In the quiet, Sylvie realized Roselle was still standing in the room. She looked up to find the young woman staring at her with a mixture of adoration and awe.

Sylvie glared at her. "*Go.*"

Roselle darted from the office.

Sylvie shook her head and sank into her soft white chair, the plush fabric molding around her hips and buttocks. She ran three profitable companies from this office, located in Atlanta atop a twenty-story building where she leased fifteen floors and part of the basement.

The entire office contained ultramodern pieces with a feminine twist, stylish but engineered for comfort. The shaggy white chair behind her desk was a very popular item she'd designed, made of ivory sheepskin resting on clear Lucite legs. It went well with the rest of the furnishings, which included white built-in shelves filled with books and awards, and a glass coffee table encircled by a sofa and two armchairs.

Her film development company funded documentaries, a line of office furniture offered high-end pieces made of hearty woods and vibrant fabrics for female executives, and she sold fashion and cosmetics products under the Sylvie brand. She was proud of her accomplishments, but particularly the makeup line, created for women with darker skin tones. Made from natural and organic ingredients, the line had won numerous awards. Reviewers raved that they often forgot they were wearing makeup and swore the products improved their complexions.

She found her notes and scribbled a few items onto her pad, and then went to work drafting a memo on her laptop. Approximately twenty minutes into the task, the intercom beeped.

The voice of her administrative assistant, Inez, came through the speaker. "You have a visitor."

Sylvie lifted a brow at the guarded tone. Her eyes skirted away from the document on the computer to the phone on the corner of her desk. "Who is it?"

"Your ex-husband. Oscar Brooks."

She stiffened.

What was Oscar doing at her office? She couldn't recall the last time he'd been there. Certainly not since they'd divorced and she moved to this new location when her businesses expanded.

With all of their children grown, they had little reason to communicate with each other, and the last time she saw him had been a month ago. They had both attended a function in Miami where their daughter gave a speech. Oscar showed up with one of his young girlfriends, a slight Sylvie made sure he knew she didn't appreciate. They'd had another confrontation when they saw each other at breakfast in the hotel restaurant the next morning, and that had been the last time she'd seen him.

"Miss Johnson, are you there? Should I send him in or…?"

"One moment."

Sylvie went to the gilded oval mirror hanging on the wall and checked her appearance. Perfect. Her raven hair was pulled back from her face, covered in neutral-toned foundation and lipstick to match her dark brown skin.

She straightened the hem of her sleeveless royal blue peplum top and smoothed a hand down the front of the canary trousers before stalking over to the desk. She didn't really care what Oscar thought, but still wanted to look her best. "Send him in."

Sylvie stood behind the desk, posed with a hand on her hip, and took a slow breath, quietly easing air into her lungs as she awaited her ex-husband's entrance.

Oscar entered slowly, dressed in black loafers, jeans, and a dark pullover. His eyes took in the bright room, sun-drenched from the windows covered with sheer drapes at her back, highlighting the white, tan, and splashes of pale rose that filled the expansive room.

The patch of gray hair over his right temple hinted at his age, a man in his fifties. His mother was Brazilian, his father African-American. Some recognized his Latin roots; others mistook the curly hair and swarthy skin for someone of Middle Eastern descent.

He was the kind of person who did his own thing and didn't care what other people thought. One of the many reasons she'd been attracted to him in the first place. He'd been so different from the well-mannered young men she knew that he'd immediately intrigued her.

But right now Sylvie was not intrigued. In fact, she was annoyed because he had disrupted her day.

"You need to shave," she told him, casting a disparaging eye at the shadow of whiskers that covered his chin and jaw. *And a haircut,* she added silently, critically assessing the loose curls on his head. Her eyes avoided the hint of chest hair revealed by the three open buttons on his shirt, and she kept her body still to combat the faint flutter of warmth that seeped into her chest at the untamed virility of his appearance.

Oscar rubbed his palm across the hairs on his jaw, peppered with gray. "I'm my own man. I can do what I want. Have been able to do what I've wanted for fifteen glorious years." He sent a tight smile in her direction.

He crossed his arms over his chest, revealing defined biceps. According to the children, he stayed in shape by regularly going out on his boat. It was obvious he spent a lot of time out there. His face was weathered and sun-kissed from being out in the sun, but he was still very much the young man she had fallen in love with. With a sparkle to his dark brown eyes, and quite handsome.

And she wished she hadn't noticed.

Her nostrils flared. "What do you want?"

"I came to extend an olive branch." He came further

into the room, and the skin on Sylvie's neck tightened upon his approach.

"Why?" she asked.

"No need to sound so suspicious. I'm worried about our children, and I want to talk to you about them. Mind if I sit?"

"I'm very busy—"

He dropped into the chair in front of the desk and crossed an ankle over his knee.

"Excuse me, but what are you doing?" Sylvie asked.

"Have a seat, Sylvie, and let's talk."

"Why should I talk to you?"

"Because the only thing you love more than money is our children. They're the only good thing that came out of our marriage, wouldn't you agree?"

The barb sent a razor-sharp pain through her chest, and Sylvie dropped her gaze to the glass top desk. Regrouping, she compressed her lips and recovered, steeling herself for the conversation with her ex.

She coolly looked at Oscar. "I agree. They're the only good thing."

She sat down across from him.

ALSO BY DELANEY DIAMOND

More stories with mature couples!

Passion Rekindled (Brooks Family #2). Oscar Brooks has always assumed that his ex-wife hates him, but after an unplanned kiss, he's not so sure. Why does Sylvie Johnson always have such a hostile response to his presence? Is it love, or is it hate? He's determined to find out.

Seasoned. Three women. One summer. After three failed marriages, Renee Joseph is through with men, then things heat up with her neighbor. Right when Adelaide Flores is getting used to life without her ex-husband, they're thrown a curve ball that forces them together and reminds her of how much she still misses him. All her adult life, Jackie Bryant's happiness will depend on the tough decision she must make when her old lover, Tyson, comes back into her life.

ABOUT THE AUTHOR

Delaney Diamond is the USA Today Bestselling Author of sweet, sensual, passionate romance novels. Originally from the U.S. Virgin Islands, she now lives in Atlanta, Georgia. She reads romance novels, mysteries, thrillers, and a fair amount of nonfiction. When she's not busy reading or writing, she's in the kitchen trying out new recipes, dining at one of her favorite restaurants, or traveling to an interesting locale.

Enjoy free reads and the first chapter of all her novels on her website. Join her mailing list to get sneak peeks, notices of sale prices, and find out about new releases.

Join her mailing list
www.delaneydiamond.com

facebook.com/DelaneyDiamond
twitter.com/DelaneyDiamond
instagram.com/authordelaneydiamond
bookbub.com/authors/delaney-diamond
pinterest.com/delaneydiamond

www.ingramcontent.com/pod-product-compliance
Lightning Source LLC
Chambersburg PA
CBHW022024170626
46808CB00003B/1048